The Land of Promise
The Seven Seals

Secret Societies and the Sisterhood Sleuths

Cathy Warshaw

All illustrations (interior) by Oksana Ponomar

ISBN: 979-8-218-99220-0 (paperback)
ISBN: 979-8-899-01760-5 (ebook)

Disclaimer

This book is a work of fiction. While some locations, events, and individuals are inspired by actual events, places, and figures, all characters have been fictionalized. The events depicted in this story are entirely fictional. For all other characters, any resemblance to real persons, living or deceased, is purely coincidental and unintentional.

To my dear family and friends in Israel,
Your warmth, resilience, and spirit inspire me every day.
Through this story, I hope to share Israel, not just as a place
but as a land of extraordinary people—diverse, kind,
and full of life.
It is my privilege to honor your perseverance and joy.
This book is a tribute to your spirit,
and I am forever grateful for your love
and the memories we share.

To join the
Secret Societies and the Sisterhood Sleuths club
go to
https://www.sisterhoodsleuths.net, or
https://www.sisterhoodsleuths.blog

CONTENTS

Prologue

The Obsidian Eye was behind them now, its power temporarily neutralized but far from forgotten. The underground chamber they had returned to still echoed with the memories of their earlier frantic search, each step they'd taken then marking the beginning of a new chapter. It had been important to come back to retrieve a key clue to what was coming next. Chloe stood in the center of the group, clutching the fragile parchment they had risked coming back for. Her eyes scanned its faded Hebrew script once more, the gravity of their discovery settling like a weight on her chest.

The others gathered around her, their expressions a mixture of exhaustion and determination. Lily's eyes sparkled with curiosity. Gil, leaning against a crumbling column with his leather jacket slung over his shoulder, studied the parchment with his sharp brown eyes, his mind already calculating their next move.

"This has to be it," Chloe said, her voice steady but quiet. "The Seven Seals mentioned here … they're connected to The Land of Promise. It's Israel."

Thalia, the group's translator and historian, adjusted her glasses, her olive-toned skin glistening with sweat. "The symbols align with ancient texts I've seen before," she said, her voice tinged with awe. "This isn't just a clue—it's a map. The Society has been searching for these seals to unlock … something. Something dangerous."

Yuki's quiet intensity drew their attention next. "If they succeed," she said, her Japanese accent soft but firm, "they'll have power over forces we don't yet understand." Her hand rested on the sleek case she carried, her engineering tools always at the ready.

Mei spoke up, her sharp voice cutting through the tension. "We'll need to act fast. If The Society's already on their way to Israel, they'll be preparing for us." Her dark eyes gleamed with determination, her background in biochemistry lending an edge of practicality to her words.

Luca smirked, his Italian accent laced with his usual arrogance. "If they think they can hide, they're wrong.

I'll find their digital trails, no matter how deep they bury them."

Aoife, the geospatial analyst, crossed her arms and tilted her head. "It won't just be about finding them. If the seals are hidden underground or within ancient ruins, we'll need to know the land better than they do. That's where I come in."

Chloe turned to Seraphine, the enigmatic woman with green eyes that burned with a quiet intensity and black hair streaked with silver. "And you?" Chloe asked.

Seraphine's voice was low but resolute. "I know The Society's methods. If they're after the Seven Seals, I'll know how to anticipate their moves. But make no mistake … they won't let us get close without a fight."

Chloe nodded, folding the parchment carefully and slipping it into her bag. "Then it's settled. We're going to Israel. We need to find these seals, stop The Society, and make sure they never use this power."

The group exchanged determined glances, their diverse talents and united resolve binding them together. The Land of Promise awaited, and with it, the promise of answers—and danger.

As they began to leave the chamber, the faint echoes of their footsteps carried with them the weight of what lay ahead. The battle against The Society was far from over, and this time, the stakes were higher than ever.

Chapter 1

The Trip to Israel

The hum of the airplane engines was a steady backdrop to the lively atmosphere inside the cabin. Unlike the usual hush of international flights, this one buzzed with energy—chatter, laughter, the crinkle of snack wrappers being passed around. It felt more like a road trip with friends than a long-haul flight.

Chloe pressed her forehead to the window, mesmerized by the endless blue sky stretching beyond the wing. Her younger sister, Lily, had already made a friend: an elderly woman with bright eyes and a warm smile, who had just handed her a small package of homemade pastries. "You must visit Jaffa," the woman insisted. "The markets are alive with color, and the sea looks like it was painted by the gods themselves."

"We'll try to!" Lily grinned, taking a bite. "Oh wow, these are amazing. What's in them?"

Across the aisle, Gil sat with his laptop open, but even he was distracted by the infectious warmth in the cabin. A stocky man with the distinct accent of a Russian Israeli leaned over. "First time to Israel?" he asked.

Gil nodded. "I'm Israeli, but my friends are visiting for the first time."

"Ah," the man chuckled. "They are in for an adventure. They must see the Negev Desert. There is nowhere on earth like it."

Further down, Seraphine's sharp green eyes scanned the rows of passengers. Even in this friendly setting, she remained alert. A young Arab Israeli couple sitting beside her offered a small bag of almonds. "For the road," the woman said kindly.

Seraphine accepted with a small nod. "Thank you."

The group was awestruck by the diversity around them—families with toddlers, solo backpackers, and professionals returning home. The differences in culture, language, and background somehow made the space feel richer, like they were stepping into a world much bigger than themselves.

As the plane began its descent, passengers eagerly pointed out landmarks.

"That's Tel Aviv," a young man told Chloe, nodding toward the shimmering city below. "The beating heart of modern Israel."

When they landed, they were swept into the organized chaos of Ben Gurion Airport. The mix of languages—Hebrew, Arabic, Russian, and English—created a kind of music. Soldiers stood in clusters, their rifles slung over their shoulders, their eyes sharp but not unkind.

"Why so many soldiers?" Lily whispered to Gil, eyes wide.

Gil smiled reassuringly. "Security is second nature here. If someone leaves a bag unattended, it is reported in seconds. No risks are taken."

Chloe spotted a soldier calmly directing a lost traveler and was struck by the contrast—vigilance balanced with kindness.

A tall man with Gil's sharp brown eyes and an easy smile was waiting for them. "Welcome to Israel!" he called, waving.

"Aaron!" Gil broke into a rare grin. "Everyone, this is my cousin Aaron."

Aaron greeted them with firm handshakes. "I've got a bus waiting, stocked with cold drinks. Let's get you out of this heat."

The drive to Jerusalem was a blur of winding roads and lively conversation. They arrived in the German Colony, a neighborhood with cobbled streets and stone houses that felt like it belonged in a storybook.

Their guesthouse, Haus Morgenstern, was announced with an old wooden sign and a welcoming glow from the windows. A man and woman emerged to greet them, their smiles as warm as the evening air.

"Shalom!" The man's German accent was still noticeable despite years in Israel. He was in his late 60s, with silver hair neatly combed back and round glasses perched on his nose. "I'm Klaus Morgenstern, and this is my wife, Ingrid."

Ingrid, petite with wavy blonde hair, extended her hand. "We're so happy to have you here. Please, come in."

Inside, the air smelled of fresh bread. The wooden floors gleamed under antique chandeliers, and framed photos of old Jerusalem lined the walls. A large bunch of bright red anemones—Israel's national flower—was tastefully arranged on the entrance hall table next to a sign-in register.

"This is your home while you're here," Klaus said warmly. "Feel free to relax anywhere."

"Breakfast is from seven to nine," Ingrid added. "We make fresh breads and jams. And of course, Israeli breakfasts are unforgettable."

"Sounds perfect," Chloe murmured, already picturing slow mornings with good coffee.

Klaus led them upstairs to their rooms. "We've added safes for your peace of mind."

While the rest of the team went their separate ways to their assigned rooms, Gil accompanied Lily and Chloe to the one they would share.

The rooms were simple but charming. Crisp white linens covered the twin beds, and a small window overlooked the street below. Fresh flowers rested on the nightstand. It was cozy, but more than that, it felt safe.

"This is lovely," Lily said sincerely.

"And if you need anything," Klaus added, "we're just downstairs."

As the door closed behind them, Gil leaned against the doorframe, watching the sisters take it all in. "What do you think?"

"It's perfect," Chloe admitted.

"Thanks for staying with us, Gil," Lily said, glancing at him.

He shrugged, ever casual. "It's what I'm here for."

Chloe met his gaze. For the first time in days, she felt grounded, like maybe, just maybe, they were exactly where they needed to be.

Chapter 2

Dawn of Discovery

The morning sunlight streamed through the lace curtains of the guesthouse dining room, casting intricate patterns across the polished wooden floors. The room hummed with the sounds of clinking plates, the rustling of newspapers, and the low murmur of conversation as the group gathered for breakfast.

The sight before them was nothing short of a feast. The long wooden table overflowed with vibrant colors and enticing aromas tickled their appetites: freshly baked challah, golden and soft, flaky pastries dusted with powdered sugar, and an array of spreads—creamy tahini, zesty labneh, and an assortment of homemade jams bursting with fruit. Bowls of sun-ripened fruits, from plump pomegranates to figs oozing with sweetness, stood beside plates of crisp cucumbers, juicy tomatoes, and bright bell peppers. Nestled among them were dishes of olives and fresh mint, their scents mingling with the rich aroma of strong black coffee. The selection of eggs—hard-boiled, scrambled with fragrant herbs, and perfectly poached—was accompanied by smoked fish, including delicate slices of salmon and rich, flavorful mackerel.

Lily's eyes widened as she reached for a piece of bread. "Okay, this is next-level amazing. I think I might actually cry."

Klaus, pouring coffee into tiny cups, chuckled. "Israeli breakfasts are legendary for a reason. Eat up. You'll need the energy."

As the group settled in, their lighthearted chatter gradually shifted to the reason they had come. Over the clatter of silverware, Chloe set down her fork, her blue eyes serious. "Let's go over what we know. The Society isn't some new enemy. They've been hiding in the shadows for generations."

Aaron who had arrived early to join them for breakfast, nodded grimly. "They claim to be the guardians of history, but they're just hoarders of knowledge, twisting the past to fit their own agenda."

Thalia leaned forward. "They aren't just treasure hunters with fancy degrees. They've embedded themselves in governments, academia, and even intelligence agencies. Their reach is longer than we ever imagined."

Gil folded his arms. "The Obsidian Eye was only the tip of the iceberg. We saw how far they were willing to go to control artifacts with ancient power. The Seven Seals? That's a whole different level. If they get their hands on them, we're looking at a world rewritten in their image."

Seraphine's voice was calm, but a warning lingered beneath it. "They won't hesitate. If they control the seals, they control something that could shift the balance of power. And they have no conscience about using it."

Luca leaned back, tapping his fingers against the table. "And let's not forget—they don't play fair. We've already seen what they do to people who stand in their way. Historians disappearing, evidence wiped off the face of the earth. And now? Kidnapping."

The weight of their mission settled over the table, the unspoken burden pressing against their shoulders.

Aaron exhaled and cleared his throat. "I hope you're ready. I've arranged a safe place for us to meet."

Chloe arched an eyebrow. "Where?"

"A secluded house nearby," Aaron said. "It's quiet, secure, and has everything we need to work without interruption."

After breakfast, they loaded onto the bus. The ride took them through Jerusalem's winding streets until they reached a modest stone house tucked away at the end of a narrow lane. Ivy climbed its walls, and the garden was wild with vibrant flowers and fragrant herbs. The atmosphere inside was peaceful, with soft lighting and comfortable furniture arranged around a large central table.

Aaron had thought of everything. The fridge was stocked with fresh juices, bottled water, and soda, while bowls of snacks—nuts, dried fruit, and crackers—sat waiting on the side table.

Gil gave a nod of approval. "This'll do."

Aaron smirked. "Figured you'd like it. Now, let's talk next steps."

As they gathered around the table, Aaron began. "We need to focus on the Western Wall and the tunnels beneath it. The Society is probably already sniffing around. We have to be quick and quiet."

The group leaned in as Aaron laid out the details. "The tunnels run along the base of the Western Wall, accessing underground structures hidden for thousands of years. Some passages are narrow, others open into massive chambers with ancient artifacts and inscriptions. It's the perfect place for The Society to search."

Thalia nodded. "Originally, these tunnels were just an archaeological site, but they've revealed much more—ancient streets, ritual baths, even hidden reservoirs. If the seals have any connection to sacred sites, this would be the ideal place for The Society to dig."

Luca tapped the table. "And security?"

"Tight," Aaron admitted. "Parts of the tunnels are open to guided tours, but some sections are completely off-limits. We'll need to figure out how to get in without raising suspicion. Yuki, your skills will be crucial."

Yuki nodded, her sharp mind already at work. "I need to see the security setup firsthand. Cameras, sensors … anything they've got."

Seraphine's green eyes darkened. "And The Society? If they're already in the tunnels, we'll run into them."

Aaron sighed. "That's a risk we have to take. The tunnels are vast, though. If we move carefully, we might have the advantage."

Mei finally spoke. "If The Society is searching for something, they'll leave traces—subtle disturbances, excavation sites. I can track their movements."

Chloe nodded, her voice firm. "We have the right team for this. Let's strategize and make it happen."

When their meeting concluded, Aaron stood. "Before we dive in, my mother has lunch waiting for us. She's been eager to meet you all."

The ride to Aaron's home was short but scenic. The streets of Jerusalem pulsed with life: street vendors selling fragrant spices, musicians playing in quiet corners, and families laughing together. His home was warm, filled with towering bookshelves, ancient artifacts, and the rich aroma of a home-cooked meal.

Dr. Rachel Levine greeted them at the door, regal yet inviting. "Welcome," she said, her smile kind. "I've heard so much about you all."

Lunch was nothing short of spectacular—slow-cooked lamb, vibrant salads, fragrant rice, and pastries that melted in their mouths. Laughter and conversation filled the air, a brief respite before they stepped back into the shadows of history.

As they ate, they knew one thing for certain: the real adventure was just beginning.

Chapter 3

Secrets Beneath the Stones

The scent of roasted lamb and herbs filled the air, mingling with the faint tang of parchment and ancient stone. Dr. Rachel Levine's home was a perfect blend of modern comfort and historical richness, reflecting her life's passion. Sleek furniture sat alongside shelves crammed with books, old scrolls, and artifacts she had collected over the years. The dining table—a sturdy, carved cedar piece—bore the marks of years of study sessions, family meals, and discussions like this one.

The group gathered around, finishing up their meal. Despite their disparate backgrounds, the shared past adventure had created something of a bond between them and a quiet sense of camaraderie was developing, now including Aaron and Dr. Levine. Chloe and Lily sat side by side, Chloe's sharp blue eyes scanning the room while Lily absently twirled a strand of her always unruly hair. Across from them, Gil leaned back, his bag slung over the back of his chair, observing with quiet intensity. Luca, ever animated, gestured enthusiastically as he shared a humorous story, his Italian accent adding flair to every word. Yuki, Mei, Aoife, Seraphine, Thalia, and Aaron rounded out the group, each bringing their own expertise to the table.

Dr. Levine, a woman in her sixties with sharp hazel eyes and graying curls, stood to clear the dishes. Her movements were brisk and efficient, honed from years of working in her field. "Leave those," Chloe said, starting to stand.

"Nonsense," Dr. Levine waved a hand dismissively. "You're my guests. Sit, sit. The real work begins after the meal, doesn't it?"

"Indeed it does," Aoife rumbled, her Irish accent adding warmth. "But I'd not mind a bit of dessert first."

Dr. Levine chuckled. "There's baklava in the kitchen. Help yourselves. We'll move to the sitting area once you're ready."

Minutes later, they reconvened in the living room. Maps, notes, and old photographs were spread across the coffee table. Dr. Levine took a deep breath before speaking, her gaze serious. "I've spent decades studying this land," she said. "Jerusalem is a city of layers, each civilization building upon the ruins of the last. Every stone here tells a story—some louder than others."

She glanced at Aaron, who nodded, picking up where she left off. "My mother specializes in uncovering buried histories. She has led excavations across Israel, including Megiddo, Masada, and Qumran. But recently, her work has focused on something bigger—hidden sites that The Society might exploit."

Lily leaned forward, her curiosity piqued. "What exactly have you found?"

Dr. Levine held up a photograph of a fragment of an ornate tablet etched with unfamiliar symbols. "This," she said, passing it around. "It was uncovered near the Old City—an area previously considered insignificant. The writing combines ancient Hebrew, Aramaic, and something I can't quite place."

Luca studied the image. "Could be a cipher."

"Possibly," Dr. Levine agreed. "That's where I hoped someone with your skill set could help."

Luca grinned. "If it's a code, I'll crack it."

"The complexity here suggests something ancient," Seraphine noted, her melodic voice thoughtful. "I've studied inscriptions from various secretive groups—this might be tied to an older network."

Aaron adjusted his glasses. "If The Society has been using the tunnels beneath the Western Wall, they could be storing artifacts or hiding messages in plain sight."

Chloe and Lily exchanged glances. "We've seen before how they layer secrets," Chloe said. "If we want to find anything, we must think like they do."

Lily nodded. "It's not just about what's there—it's about how they would hide it."

"What about structural integrity?" Yuki asked. "If these tunnels are old, they could be dangerous. I can bring scanners to detect weak points before we go in."

Mei leaned forward. "And I can analyze biological traces. I can extract information if The Society left anything organic—paper, fabric, even fingerprints. If we want to find out who they are or where they've been, this might come in handy?"

Aoife tapped the map in front of them. "The tunnels' layout will be key. I've mapped underground structures before. I can find areas that might be hiding something."

Gil, who had been listening quietly, finally spoke. "We need to anticipate defenses. Even if The Society isn't there now, they've likely set up traps or misdirections." He looked at Dr. Levine. "Auntie, do you have blueprints or historical records of the tunnels?"

Dr. Levine sighed. "Some. But they're incomplete. I've pieced together as much as possible from historical records, but many documents were lost over the centuries."

"That's fine," Gil said. "Gaps just mean room for discovery."

For the next hour, the group reviewed maps and discussed strategies.

Yuki outlined her approach to navigating structural hazards, while Mei explained the tools she'd bring for biological analysis. Aoife traced the best routes to take, using the historical records to adjust what the maps initially indicated. Seraphine planned to cross-reference symbols and markings with her research, and Aaron made a checklist of logistical needs for the expedition.

"We need more than just a plan," Gil finally said, tapping his fingers against his laptop. We need leverage. Auntie, do you have contacts who could get us access to restricted areas?"

Dr. Levine nodded. "A few. I'll make some calls tonight. Meanwhile, I'll prepare a list of what you'll need. The tunnels are unforgiving—even for experienced explorers."

Chloe hesitated before asking, "What about you? Will you come with us?"

Dr. Levine smiled faintly. "I'm not as young as I used to be. Maybe later."

The evening stretched on as the group solidified their plans. When they finally stood to leave, Dr. Levine walked them to the door, the warm light of her home casting long shadows on the street outside.

"Good luck," she said. "And remember, history isn't just in books. It's in the stones beneath our feet. Keep your eyes open."

Chloe turned back to nod, a silent promise passing between them. Tomorrow would bring challenges, but tonight, they had a plan and trusted one another.

Chapter 4

The Mystical Rabbi and the Streets of Mea She'arim

The tension in the safehouse was thick, curling around them like smoke. Chloe ran her fingers over the worn parchment spread across the table, its rough texture sending a chill up her spine. The cryptic Hebrew text and geometric symbols pulsed with mystery, silently whispering secrets only the dead could hear.

Lily leaned in, her brow furrowed. "It almost looks like a map," she murmured, tracing the intricate tree-like diagram with one finger. "But a map to what?"

Gil stood by the window, arms crossed; he'd been pacing like a caged wolf. His laptop bag was slung across his chest, his perpetual weapon of choice. Across the room, Aaron sat cross-legged, flipping through a thick, dusty book that smelled of mildew and history. He occasionally sneezed as he disturbed centuries of dust.

"It's got to be connected to the Sefirot," Chloe muttered, pointing at the diagram. "The ten attributes in Kabbalah, which is a mystical branch of Judaism. But what does it mean?"

Gil suddenly stopped. His sharp eyes locked onto the parchment, and something clicked into place. "Mea She'arim," he said.

Chloe blinked. "What?"

"It's a reference to an ultra-Orthodox neighborhood not far from here," Gil explained. "These symbols belong to a specific sect—very private, very old-world. If there are answers, they're buried there."

Aaron shook his head. "Not this time. You and Chloe would stand out too much." His voice was firm, apologetic. "They don't take kindly to outsiders. Especially women. We need to blend in."

Chloe bristled, frustration flashing in her blue eyes. She hated being sidelined. "So, what? You and Gil just waltz in and they spill their secrets?"

Gil smirked. "Not exactly." He hesitated for a beat. "But I know someone. A rabbi."

Luca leaned back against the wall, arms folded, the usual cocky grin tugging at his lips. "Even Special Forces need a rabbi, huh?"

Gil didn't answer. He just grabbed his coat.

Disguising for the Mission

The next morning, Aaron stood in front of the mirror, pulling at the collar of his crisp white shirt. "I look ridiculous."

Gil, already dressed in full disguise—black hat, *tzitzit*, and long coat—gave him an appraising look. "You look the part. Which means you'll survive."

Aaron tugged at the fake peyot attached to his hair. "This is humiliating."

"Think of it as deep cover," Gil said, tucking a Hebrew Bible under his arm. "Or pretend you're in a historical reenactment."

Aaron shot him a glare. "Remind me why I agreed to this?"

Gil shrugged, grinning. "Because you're the only one who can keep up."

Aaron sighed. "Great. No pressure."

Entering Mea She'arim

Walking into Mea She'arim felt like stepping through a portal into another era.

The narrow streets twisted into a maze of cobblestone alleys, flanked by old stone buildings, their shutters closed against the modern world. Hebrew and Yiddish posters fluttered on the walls—some religious, some warning against the dangers of secular influences.

Men in long black coats and wide-brimmed hats strode past, their expressions solemn, their voices low as they debated theology and law. Women in headscarves and wigs moved quickly, shepherding young children, their whispers blending into the distant hum of prayer.

The air smelled of fresh challah, burning wood, and something deeper—something ancient.

Aaron kept his head down and murmured to Gil, "I feel like an extra in *Fiddler on the Roof*."

"Keep your voice low," Gil muttered back. "Just nod if someone looks at you."

Aaron nodded solemnly at a passing man, who barely acknowledged him. "This is the weirdest op I've ever been on," he muttered.

Gil led them through the winding streets until they reached a small stone house, slightly set apart. A polished mezuzah gleamed on the doorframe.

Gil knocked three times in a precise rhythm.

The door creaked open.

The Mystical Rabbi

The world seemed to hush as Rav Eliyahu appeared in the doorway.

He was old—ageless, really—his long white beard flowing over his chest. His piercing blue eyes burned with an intensity that made Aaron feel like the man could read every thought he'd ever had.

Candlelight flickered inside, casting long shadows over ancient bookshelves groaning under the weight of forgotten knowledge. Scrolls lined the walls, their edges curling with time. A single candle burned on the wooden desk, wax dripping like slow tears.

Rav Eliyahu studied them for a long moment before stepping aside, silently inviting them in.

"You seek answers," he said, his voice like rustling parchment.

Gil nodded. "We need your guidance. This is about The Society."

The rabbi's expression darkened. "Dangerous men," he murmured. "They twist sacred knowledge for their own gain."

Aaron leaned forward. "Where are they meeting?"

Rav Eliyahu hesitated. Then, he reached for a scroll, his hands steady despite his age. He unfurled it carefully, tracing a passage written in Aramaic.

"After your call, I looked into what you told me about that parchment you have. The Dome of the Rock," he whispered.

Aaron's stomach clenched. The golden-domed shrine was one of the holiest places on Earth.

"They will gather there under the cover of night," the rabbi continued. "But to spy on them is to invite great danger."

Gil's jaw tightened. "We don't have a choice."

The rabbi closed his eyes as if listening to something beyond their understanding. "The seals are not mere relics," he said at last. "They are conduits of energy. Their alignment with the sacred geometry of this land is no accident."

He traced a symbol onto parchment—a circle within a triangle, surrounded by glyphs.

"The balance of these forces is delicate," he warned. "If disrupted, the consequences could be beyond comprehension."

Aaron swallowed. "What happens if they succeed?"

The rabbi's gaze turned to steel.

"The gates will open. But not to what they expect."

A gust of wind rattled the shutters. The candle flame flickered violently, casting eerie shadows along the walls.

The rabbi folded the parchment and pressed it into Gil's hands.

"You must be cautious. And you must not go alone."

Returning to the Safehouse

When Gil and Aaron returned, the team was waiting.

Chloe's arms were crossed. "Well?"

Gil placed the parchment on the table, his expression grim. "The Society is meeting at the Dome of the Rock."

Lily's eyes widened. "That's one of the most sacred places in the world."

"Exactly," Aaron said. "Underneath it is the Foundation Stone—believed to be the place where heaven and earth connect. If The Society is there, they aren't just after power. They're trying to manipulate something ancient."

Chloe inhaled sharply. "How do we get close?"

Aaron grinned, his earlier discomfort forgotten. "That's where the fun begins."

Gil frowned and added, "The rabbi said something about sacred geometry and the seals. That's not a coincidence."

Seraphine finally spoke. "Some believe ancient sites form an energy grid. If The Society understands this, they aren't just chasing relics. They're trying to control something *bigger*."

Silence settled over the room, pregnant with the implications.

Chloe exhaled, determination flickering in her blue eyes. "Then we'd better get there first."

The candle on the table flickered, an eerie echo of what Gil and Aaron had just seen back with the rabbi. The race had begun.

Chapter 5

The Hidden Chamber

The tunnels stretched before them, dark and damp, smelling of earth and centuries of time. Chloe stepped carefully, feeling the rough, uneven stones beneath her boots. The air was close, pressing in around them.

Behind her, Luca's tablet cast a faint glow, their shadows stretching like ghosts against the ancient walls. "Man, I feel like we're about to trigger some Indiana Jones booby trap," he muttered.

"Don't jinx us," Lily shot back, adjusting the strap of her bag.

Gil moved with quiet confidence, his leather jacket creaking slightly with each step. His sharp eyes scanned every inch of the passage, instincts honed by years in the field. Yuki and Mei followed in precise, calculated steps, their expressions unreadable but their senses on high alert.

Aoife had to squeeze through a particularly tight section, muttering, "If this tunnel gets any smaller, I'll be digging my way through with my bare hands."

Seraphine barely made a sound, her gaze absorbing everything.

The tunnel suddenly widened into a circular stone chamber.

"This is it," Luca whispered, excitement crackling in his voice. He aimed his tablet at the walls. "Look at these markings."

Chloe moved closer, running her fingers over the ancient symbols carved deep into the stone. The cold surface hummed beneath her touch. "It's some kind of writing," she murmured. "Yuki, can you figure it out?"

Yuki adjusted her glasses and pulled out a small scanner. The device hummed softly as she moved it over the engravings. "It's old—really old. This isn't just Hebrew. It's mixed with something else. Maybe Aramaic, maybe something even older."

"We don't have time," Gil interrupted, his tone edged with urgency. His body was taut, scanning the room like a soldier waiting for the first shot to fire. "If The Society knows we're here, they'll be coming."

Lily frowned, hands on her hips. "This place is too well-hidden for it to be just a bunch of wall carvings. There's gotta be more."

"She's right," Mei agreed, stepping forward. "People don't go through this much effort just to write on walls. This chamber was meant to *hide* something."

Chloe's gaze fell to the floor. "What about these grooves?" She crouched, tracing them with her fingers. "It almost looks like a map … or a mechanism."

Aoife knelt beside her, brushing the dust away. "It's a locking system," she confirmed, her voice tinged with admiration. "If we figure it out, we might just unlock whatever they were trying to protect."

Luca's fingers flew across his tablet. "If it's mechanical, there could be a power source. Let me—" His eyes lit up. "There it is. A sensor buried in the stone."

"I've got this," Yuki said, already pulling out a sleek, handheld device. She connected a thin cable, her fingers moving swiftly.

A low rumble shook the ground. Dust rained down from the ceiling as golden light pulsed through the grooves in the floor.

Chloe and Lily exchanged a glance, their hearts pounding.

Then, with a deep, grinding noise, the stone slid away, revealing a spiraling staircase descending into the darkness.

"Well, that looks *welcoming*," Gil muttered, pulling out a flashlight. "Shall we?"

The Hidden Chamber Below

They moved cautiously, the air growing colder as they descended. The stone walls felt closer, pressing in around them.

At the bottom, the chamber widened into a room filled with strange artifacts—scrolls encased in protective glass, metallic tools with intricate etchings, vials of unknown substances that glowed faintly in the dim light.

"This is it," Mei whispered, her breath hitching. "This is what The Society has been hiding. They've been at this through time for generations."

In the center of the room stood a stone pedestal. On it, resting like something out of legend, was a round artifact covered in delicate carvings. The surface pulsed with a faint, golden glow.

"The first seal," Luca breathed. His usual cocky attitude was gone, replaced with sheer awe. "It's real."

"And dangerous," Mei added, stepping closer. "If the legends are true, these seals hold enormous power."

Gil's hand went instinctively to his weapon. "Then we need to secure it before The Society—"

The chamber trembled.

A hidden door burst open.

Figures in black stormed in.

The Fight for the First Seal

"DOWN!" Gil's voice cut through the chaos like a gunshot.

In a blur of movement, he yanked Chloe and Lily behind a stone pillar just as an attacker lunged at them. Gil spun, fluid and lethal, catching the man's wrist and twisting it with expert precision. A second later, the attacker crumpled, unconscious.

Yuki and Mei sprang into action. Yuki sidestepped a blow, grabbed her attacker's wrist, and twisted hard.

With a sweep of her leg, she sent him crashing to the ground.

Mei's movements were almost graceful, her training evident as she ducked beneath a strike and delivered a perfectly placed kick to the ribs, sending her opponent skidding back.

Seraphine was a ghost. A dagger flashed in her hand, and before the enemy even realized what was happening, she had already disabled two of them, their weapons clattering to the floor.

Luca had his back to the pedestal, shielding the artifact as best as he could. "Uh, guys? *Kind* of a lot of them!"

Gil took out another attacker, then snapped his head toward Thalia. "Now!"

Thalia had been studying the chamber's controls, hands moving quickly across an ancient-looking panel. At his command, she pressed a glowing symbol.

A sudden pulse of energy shot out, crackling through the air. The attackers staggered back, momentarily stunned.

"It won't hold them for long," Gil warned.

"Then we run," Chloe said firmly.

With the first seal secured, they bolted up the spiraling staircase. Their footsteps echoed behind them, mingling with the growing sounds of pursuit.

Chloe's heart hammered but fear no longer consumed her.

They had the first of the Seven Seals.

Now, they had to protect it. And themselves.

Their journey was only beginning.

And the stakes had never been higher.

Chapter 6

A Place No One Will Find

The cave was silent except for the occasional *clink* of shifting rocks as Gil secured the first seal in its hiding place. He moved with quiet efficiency, his fingers pressing the stones into place as though sealing away a dangerous secret—because, in truth, that's exactly what he was doing.

Aaron's connections had told him about this cave – there were many scattered in the hills outside the city. They'd agreed it would be a good hiding place. It wasn't easy to find, you had to be really familiar with the area to even know how to get there, let alone access it.

"There." He straightened, brushing the dust off his hands. His dark eyes scanned the spot one last time, ensuring it was perfectly concealed. "If anyone tries to find it, they'd have to know exactly what they're looking for."

Chloe crossed her arms. "And if they *are* looking for it?"

Gil met her gaze. "Then we make sure they don't find *us*, too."

Lily gave an exaggerated shiver. "Love the whole 'mysterious and dangerous' vibe you've got going, Gil. Super comforting."

Luca smirked. "You should hear his bedtime stories. Probably something like, Once upon a time, there was a guy who didn't check his surroundings … and now he's missing."

Gil ignored him and turned to the others. "Let's move," he barked his customary phrase. We don't want to stay here longer than necessary."

They climbed out of the cave, their flashlights cutting through the darkness as they maneuvered down the rocky hills outside Jerusalem. The cool night air was thick with dust, and every loose rock underfoot made someone stumble.

Aaron was waiting by the road, leaning against the side of his bus, tossing a date into his mouth like he had all the time in the world. The headlights cast long shadows against the desert terrain.

"Took you long enough," he called. "Did you get lost, or did Luca try to sweet-talk the rocks into moving?"

Luca flashed a grin. "I'll have you know, rocks appreciate good conversation."

Aaron rolled his eyes. "Right. Just get in."

Everyone piled into the bus, each falling into their usual seats without thinking—Lily next to Chloe, Thalia and Yuki across from them, Gil near the front, arms crossed. Mei and Seraphine settled toward the middle, while Aoife sprawled across the back row, looking like someone who had just conquered an army.

Thalia took in the cluttered interior—backpacks, maps, half-empty coffee cups. "You *really* live out of this thing, huh?"

Aaron grinned as he shifted into gear. "Hey, it's either this or dealing with airport security every time I chase history."

Lily flopped into her seat, sighing dramatically. "Yeah, this has *major* 'rogue archaeologist' energy. I approve."

Chloe dropped her bag at her feet. "I don't care what it looks like. I just want sleep."

But Gil was restless. He sat up front with his gaze fixed on the road, fingers tapping lightly against his arm. He looked like he was still *there*—back in the cave, back in the mission, back in his head.

Thalia noticed. She slid into the seat near him, studying him for a moment.

"You've done this kind of thing before," she said, voice quiet but certain.

Gil smiled, but it didn't reach his eyes. "Something like it."

Behind them, Chloe leaned forward. "So, what was Special Forces *really* like?"

Gil smirked slightly. "Classified."

Lily groaned. "Ugh, that is such a *cop-out* answer."

He glanced at her in the rearview mirror, amused. "Alright, fine. A lot of training. A lot of missions. And a lot of making sure no one got left behind."

Lily nodded, thoughtful. "So basically, like us. Only, y'know, government-sanctioned."

Gil chuckled. "Something like that."

A Message in the Night

By the time they reached their guest house in the German Colony, exhaustion had set in.

The old stone building stood quietly against the night sky, its small balconies lined with potted plants, and warm yellow lights glowing from within. It felt safe, like stepping into a forgotten piece of familiar history that still breathed.

As they stepped inside, Ingrid was waiting for them. Her sharp eyes softened as she took in their tired faces.

"Ah, you're back," she said, her voice warm with familiarity. "You must be exhausted. Klaus just made fresh tea—would you like some?"

Before anyone could answer, she held out a white envelope.

"This arrived for you not long ago," she said, handing it to Gil.

A flicker of unease passed through his face as he took it. His fingers worked quickly, unfolding the note as the others crowded around.

"It's from my aunt," he murmured, scanning the message. His expression darkened. "She wants to see us. *Now.*"

Chloe blinked. "Right now? We just *got* here."

Yuki checked her watch. "It's past midnight."

Luca groaned. "Of course it is. Mysteries don't believe in business hours."

Seraphine crossed her arms. "Where are we meeting her?"

"The safehouse," Gil said, already turning toward the door.

Aaron, still standing by the bus, didn't even look surprised. "So … we're not sleeping."

Lily groaned. "Apparently not."

Aaron sighed and opened the bus doors. "Fine. Back in, adventurers. Next stop: mystery and sleep deprivation."

No one even protested. Curiosity had already won out over exhaustion. They turned right back around and piled into the bus.

As they drove through the quiet streets of Jerusalem, the significance of the night settled over them.

They had secured the first seal.

But their night was far from over.

A Meeting with Dr. Levine

When they arrived at the safehouse, Gil barely had time to knock before the door swung open.

Dr. Levine stood there, arms crossed, her sharp gaze scanning each of them in turn. Despite the hour, she looked as put together as ever—poised, unreadable.

"Come in," she said briskly. Then, seeing their tired faces, she added, "I brought food."

Lily gasped in exaggerated relief. "Bless you."

Dr. Levine's lips twitched in the barest hint of a smile as she stepped aside, revealing a table laden with fresh falafel, hummus, warm pita, and fragrant rice.

Chloe didn't even hesitate—she grabbed a plate immediately. "Okay, if this mystery comes with a late dinner, I'm *listening.*"

Dr. Levine's expression softened for a moment, watching them dig in.

But then the seriousness returned.

"Eat first," she said. "Then we talk."

Something in her tone made Chloe pause, her fork hovering over her plate.

Whatever Dr. Levine had to say …
It was going to change *everything*.

Chapter 7

Shadows Over the Holy City

The safehouse still smelled of warm spices, roasted garlic, and freshly baked pita—remnants of the late-night meal Dr. Levine had graciously provided lay discarded on the table. The team had eaten in half-dazed exhaustion, their bodies begging for rest after the long night. Now, the plates were pushed aside, and the atmosphere had shifted.

Dr. Levine stood at the head of the table, her expression grave, slicing through the room's fatigue like a blade.

"I know you're all very tired," she began, her voice steady but urgent. "But listen carefully. I've uncovered something critical."

Gil, who had been leaning back in his chair, arms crossed, immediately straightened. The slight shift in his

his posture sent a ripple of alertness through the team. "Go on," he said, his voice unreadable but razor-sharp.

Dr. Levine folded her hands on the table, her gaze sweeping over each of them.

"So as you told me on the phone when you left for the cave tonight, we know The Society is going to be gathering at the Dome of the Rock tomorrow night," she said. "But this isn't just another meeting—it's *the* moment. The one they've been working toward for years. They're moving from the shadows into execution mode."

A chill gripped the room.

"They aren't just revealing themselves to each other," she continued. "They're revealing their *final strategy*. Tomorrow night, they finalize their grip on global power. They're dividing control among their most powerful members—global financial markets, biotech, satellites, artificial intelligence. Their influence over cryptocurrency, climate manipulation, and medical technology will be *absolute*."

Yuki's fingers tightened around her tablet. "They've been positioning themselves for this," she murmured.

Dr. Levine nodded grimly. "Yes. The key players—leaders from multiple nations—aren't waiting any longer. Tomorrow night, they'll cement their roles in reshaping the world order."

Luca let out a low whistle, shaking his head. "So they're not just pulling the strings anymore. They're cutting everyone *else's* off."

Mei sat forward, her eyes sharp with thought. "And the seals?"

Dr. Levine hesitated. "That's where things get complicated."

Silence fell as everyone leaned in.

"We always assumed the seals were symbols of power—historical artifacts The Society wanted for their significance. But my research has uncovered something deeper." Her voice dropped slightly. "Every clue so far ties them to major religious sites. This isn't a coincidence. The Society doesn't just believe these seals hold historical value. *They believe they're unlocking something.*"

Seraphine exhaled, her gaze flickering to the others. "They think the seals are more than relics. They think they hold true power."

Dr. Levine met her eyes. "And if they're right, there's no telling what happens next."

The weight of her words pressed down on them, suffocating the last traces of exhaustion.

The Plan Shifts

For a long moment, no one spoke. Then, finally, Gil broke the silence.

"We're not stopping them tomorrow night."

Chloe's head snapped toward him. "*What?*"

He didn't flinch at her sharp tone. Instead, he leaned forward, forearms braced against the table, his gaze level. "Not yet."

Lily's brow furrowed. "So, we're just going to *let* them move forward?"

Gil shook his head. "No. But we don't have the numbers. We don't have enough intel. If we rush in blind, we won't just lose—we'll be handing the seals to them on a silver platter."

Aaron exhaled, rubbing a hand over his jaw. "He's right. We're outnumbered and outgunned. We don't even know how many players are on the board yet."

Chloe was still tense, but she was listening. "So what's the play?"

Gil's gaze swept over the team. "Tomorrow night, we go in to gather *everything*. Names. Locations. Weak points. We find out exactly *who* we're up against and *where* they're vulnerable."

Luca let out a slow breath. "Basically … we walk straight into the viper's nest?"

Aoife leaned back in her chair, arms crossed. "And how exactly do we walk back *out*?"

Gil's mouth twitched into something that wasn't quite a smile. "By being smarter."

Chloe folded her arms. "That's a hell of a gamble."

"It's the only move we have," Gil countered. "And it won't be forever. We gather evidence, get names, and then we bring in allies if we need them."

Aoife glanced around the table. "And after that?"

Gil's expression darkened. His voice was quiet, but it carried through the room like a gunshot.

"Then we shut them down for good. Get the rest of the seals out of their grasp."

A heavy silence followed.

Chloe let out a slow breath, rubbing her temples. "So. Tomorrow, we walk into the middle of The Society's biggest event in years … and try not to die."

Luca smirked. "Well, when you put it like *that* …"

Mei shook her head, but a small smile played at the corner of her lips. "No pressure."

Thalia leaned forward, her voice steady. "We'll need disguises. A cover story. We need to look like we *belong*."

Yuki was already typing on her tablet. "Leave that to me."

Aaron, still leaning against the doorframe, sighed. "You know, when I signed up to drive the bus, I *really* didn't think espionage would be part of the deal."

Lily grinned at him. "Welcome to our world."

Chloe reached for her water bottle, taking a deep breath. The weight of everything was pressing down, but strangely, the fear wasn't as intense as before.

This wasn't over. Not by a long shot.

Tomorrow night, they wouldn't stop The Society.

But they *would* make sure that when the time came—when they were ready—

They'd sure as hell stop whatever they were planning.

59

Chapter 8

Mapping the Battlefield

The Jerusalem sun was barely creeping over the horizon when the team dragged themselves out of bed, stiff and sleep-deprived. But exhaustion had to take a back seat—today wasn't a day for second chances.

They had less than twelve hours to prepare for a mission that could go *very* wrong.

The goal?

- Get in.
- Gather intel.
- Get out.

Simple in theory. Practically impossible in execution.

Scouting the Dome of the Rock

Gil, Chloe, Seraphine, Luca, and Aaron weaved their way through the labyrinthine streets of the Old City, their pace casual. They blended into the sea of tourists and locals heading toward the Temple Mount.

They had dressed the part—loose clothes, cameras slung around their necks, sunglasses masking keen, scanning eyes. To the untrained observer, they were just another group of travelers admiring the history.

But beneath the surface?

Every single one of them was wired with adrenaline, cataloging every doorway, pathway, security checkpoint, and potential exit route as they moved.

Then, it appeared.

The Dome of the Rock stood before them, towering and resplendent in gold, an impossible gleam under the morning sun. The intricate blue-and-gold tilework shimmered, and its Arabic calligraphy wrapped around the structure like whispered prayers.

It wasn't just a building. It was the heart of history, sitting atop one of the most contested pieces of land on Earth.

Chloe's breath caught. "It's ... *stunning.*"

Aaron gave a low whistle. "Yeah. And also one of the most well-guarded places on the planet."

Understanding the Layout

They entered through the Mughrabi Gate, the only one non-Muslims were allowed to use. The other gates—Bab al-Silsila, Bab al-Qattanin, and Bab al-Rahma—were off-limits to them, but they could be crucial in an emergency.

Inside, the marble floors reflected the soft colors spilling from stained-glass windows. The mosaics—a hypnotic swirl of blues, greens, and golds—drew the eye into a dizzying pattern of ancient craftsmanship.

At the center of it all, beneath the dome, lay the Foundation Stone—the rock believed to be:

- Where Abraham prepared to sacrifice Isaac
- Where the Prophet Muhammad ascended to heaven
- Where the First and Second Temples once stood

It was more than sacred.

It was *power.*

And The Society had chosen it for a reason.

Gil's voice was low but firm. "This will be the epicenter of their meeting tonight."

Luca took a slow, casual spin, pretending to admire the architecture while subtly scanning the security setup.

- Armed guards at tight intervals.
- Surveillance cameras discreetly mounted, red lights blinking.
- Narrow, choke-point exits—bad for escaping.

Aaron exhaled. "This place is a maze."

Gil nodded. "That's why we're here. We need to know every way in and out."

Seraphine traced her eyes over the western steps. "That leads back into the Old City—good for blending in. The east?" She glanced toward the wide-open courtyards. "Bad. Too exposed."

Chloe spoke under her breath. "So what's the plan?"

Gil's mind was already racing through options. "We won't be able to walk in like tourists tonight. Visiting hours end at 2:30 p.m., and after that, security tightens. That means we need to find another way in—one that doesn't get us caught."

Luca frowned. "You're saying we have to *sneak into* one of the most heavily guarded religious sites in the world?"

Gil shot him a look. "Yes."

Aaron ran a hand through his hair. "Alright. What are our options?"

The Plan Takes Shape

Seraphine pulled out the map they had been studying earlier. "There are eight gates into the compound, but most will be locked down at night. The ones closest to the Dome are:

- Bab al-Silsila (Chain Gate)
- Bab al-Qattanin (Cotton Merchants' Gate)
- Bab al-Rahma (Gate of Mercy)"

Chloe frowned, studying the map. "Are any of them *unguarded?*"

Aaron shook his head. "Not a chance. But that doesn't mean we can't *make* an opening."

Gil's expression darkened as he tapped the eastern side of the compound. "There's another possibility. Underground tunnels."

The team exchanged glances.

"You think there's a way *in*?" Luca asked, skeptical.

"There are ancient subterranean passages beneath the Temple Mount," Aaron explained. "Some connect to the Western Wall tunnels, others lead to archaeological sites that were sealed off decades ago. If we can find an entry point from the Old City, we might be able to move beneath the structure and come up inside."

Chloe exhaled. "And if those tunnels are collapsed or blocked?"

Gil's gaze was steady. "Then we find another way."

Aaron rubbed his jaw. "Alright. We split up this afternoon. Seraphine, Luca, and I will scout the tunnels—see if there's a way in. Gil and Chloe, you map security routes and potential weak points."

Gil nodded. "And tonight, we go in completely unseen."

Returning to the Safehouse

After another hour of observing guard shifts, mapping pathways, and noting surveillance placements, they returned to the safehouse.

Lily, Yuki, Mei, Thalia, and Aoife were already there, laptops open, maps spread out, forgotten coffee cups everywhere, half empty.

Lily glanced up as they walked in. "So? What's the verdict?"

Aaron collapsed into a chair. "Oh, you know, *minor* challenge of breaking into one of the most secure sites on the planet. Nothing crazy."

Gil folded his arms. "We have two options: the gates or the tunnels. We're testing the tunnels first."

Yuki frowned. "And if those don't work?"

Chloe flopped onto the couch. "Then we improvise."

Luca threw up his hands. "Oh, great. *Love* a good last-minute improv session when ancient religious artifacts and secret societies are involved."

Aoife raised an eyebrow. "Would you *prefer* a detailed plan where we all get caught?"

Luca considered. "... Fair point."

Mei tapped a pen against her notepad. "We need an exit plan. No matter *how* we get in, getting *out* will be even harder."

Gil nodded. "That's why we don't engage. We get in, listen, and get out. Fast."

Chloe took a deep breath. "So, this is it."

Lily grinned, stretching. "Time for some good old-fashioned breaking and entering."

Aaron groaned. "Why do I let you guys drag me into these things?"

Chloe smirked. "Because we're awesome and you love us."

Aaron sighed. "I hate that you're right."

They had their plan.

Now, they had to make it work.

Chapter 9

Tracing the Seals

Back at the Safehouse – The Search for the Seals

While the scouting team were gathering intel at the Dome of the Rock, the rest of the team—Lily, Mei, Yuki, Aoife, Thalia, and Dr. Levine—had been holed up in the safehouse, surrounded by maps, ancient texts, and enough coffee to fuel an army.

The air buzzed with urgency, the weight of history pressing down on them.

Dr. Levine stood at the center of the chaos, tapping her fingers on a yellowed map of Israel spread across the table. Her expression was sharp and calculated.

"Based on my research, the remaining six seals are likely hidden at religious sites of extreme historical significance," she said, her voice carrying the gravity of the moment. "We need to move fast."

The room stilled.

Then, like a detective stringing together clues on a conspiracy board, she pointed to six locations marked in red ink.

Prioritizing the Mission

Aoife leaned back in her chair, arms crossed. "Alright. So, we need to figure out which site we hit first."

Yuki, ever the strategist, adjusted her glasses and pulled up satellite images on her tablet. "Logically, Masada would be the hardest to reach. It's isolated, a fortress on top of a mountain. If The Society is moving fast, they'd probably start with easier terrain before tackling that."

Lily drummed her fingers against the table, thinking. "If they're after power, and they believe these seals hold some kind of religious energy, they'd go for sites that have significance across multiple faiths."

Mei nodded. "That puts Bethlehem, Hebron, and the Sea of Galilee at the top of their list."

Thalia leaned forward, eyes piercing. "Do we have proof that they've been to any of these places yet?"

Dr. Levine pulled out a stack of classified reports, her fingers moving with practiced precision. "Yes.

There have been unusual excavation activities near Qumran and

Hazor in the past six months."

A heavy silence fell over the group.

Lily's face hardened. "Then they're ahead of us."

Aoife exhaled, running a hand through her thick curls. "We're running out of time."

Dividing the Work

"Then we start planning."

They moved quickly, dividing responsibilities like a well-oiled machine.

Yuki and Mei took control of satellite data—analyzing terrain, spotting unusual activity, and tracking any movement near the sites.

Lily, Aoife, and Thalia dug into historical and geological records, searching for hidden chambers, ancient tunnels, or excavation sites that could lead them to the seals.

Dr. Levine went deep into her network, reaching out to archaeologists, informants, and trusted sources who might have heard whispers of The Society's movements.

Lily rolled up her sleeves. "Alright. Let's find these seals before The Society does."

74

Chapter 10

Into the Shadows

9:00 PM – Safehouse, Jerusalem

The atmosphere in the safehouse was thick enough to cut with a knife. The team was gearing up, checking weapons, securing earpieces, running over the plan—anything to keep their hands busy and their nerves steady.

The mission sounded simple: infiltrate, observe, escape unseen.

But they all knew better.

At the center of the room, Gil, Aaron, Seraphine, Chloe, and Luca stood ready. They were dressed in dark, nondescript clothing designed to blend into the night. Their gear was minimal: comms, concealed weapons, and sheer nerve.

Dr. Levine, who had been mostly silent throughout the evening, finally stepped forward, holding a small velvet pouch.

"Alright," she said, pulling out small silver pendants attached to black cords. "I know this might seem ridiculous, but humor me."

She handed one to each of them.

Gil turned his over in his palm. A small, hand-shaped charm with an open eye in its center.

"A Hamsa?" he asked.

"And an Evil Eye," she added, pointing to the small blue-and-white eye-shaped bead next to the Hamsa on the necklace.

Chloe smirked. "Dr. Levine, are you getting superstitious on us?"

Dr. Levine rolled her eyes. "Of course not. But these are protective charms. The Hamsa wards off negative energy, and the Evil Eye protects against curses." She hesitated, then gave a small, almost sheepish smile. "Look, I don't usually go for this kind of thing, but … it can't hurt, right?"

Aaron slipped his over his neck, grinning. "Hey, I'll take all the luck I can get."

Seraphine chuckled. "Actually, I appreciate the sentiment. Ancient wisdom and all that. And let's be real—we're going to need all the protection we can get."

Dr. Levine exhaled. "Just … don't lose them, or I'll feel personally responsible."

Gil tucked his under his shirt. "Appreciated, Auntie. Now, let's move."

At the Safehouse – Monitoring the Mission

As the infiltration team left, the others stayed behind, running their own mission.

Lily, Mei, Yuki, Aoife, Thalia, and Dr. Levine were gathered around a makeshift command center—maps, satellite images, and digital blueprints of the Temple Mount spread across the table.

Yuki adjusted her earpiece, linking up with the team's comms. "I'll be monitoring your heat signatures and movement. If there's an unusual security presence, I'll guide you around it. If you hit a trap, I'll see it before you do."

Gil's voice crackled over the speaker. "Good. Keep us posted."

Mei, hunched over a tablet, ran a thermal scan of the underground tunnels. "These tunnels haven't been used for centuries, but some are still intact. We've mapped the clearest route."

Aoife frowned at the screen. "And if it collapses on them?"

Yuki kept typing. "Then we better hope they move fast."

Lily exhaled. "We just have to trust them."

Dr. Levine gave a reassuring nod. "And trust that our work here—preparing for the next seal—is just as important."

Thalia glanced at the clock. 9:30 PM.

The countdown had begun.

10:30 PM – Entering the Tunnels

Beneath the Old City, in a narrow alley tucked behind a quiet courtyard, the infiltration team gathered around a hidden stone entryway.

Luca pried open the rusted iron grate, revealing a dark passage leading underground. A stale, earthy scent wafted up from below.

Aaron peered inside. "So … who's going first?"

Gil didn't hesitate. He stepped forward, switching on his tactical flashlight.

The narrow stone walls pressed in around them as they descended. The path twisted, sloping downward. The air was thick with dust, and every step echoed like a warning.

"Yuki, we're inside," Gil murmured into his comm.

Her voice came through crisp and clear. "Copy that. I have your position locked. Keep moving forward—about 200 meters ahead, you'll find the first split in the tunnel."

As they moved deeper, ancient inscriptions covered the walls—long-eroded Hebrew letters, symbols carved into stone, whispers of a past that refused to be erased.

Chloe ran her fingers over them. "People were down here long before us."

Seraphine nodded. "And some never made it back."

Luca smirked. "Great. Love the optimism."

Yuki's voice interrupted. "Heads up. You're reaching a fork in the tunnels. Take the left path."

Gil led them through the tight corridor, their breaths shallow as they kept moving.

11:45 PM – Emerging at the Dome of the Rock

They reached a sealed archway—ancient stones stacked tightly, blocking their way.

Aaron pressed his hand against the rock. "There should be a way through."

Luca examined the seams. "This section is newer. Someone sealed it off recently."

Gil didn't hesitate. He pulled out a small charge from his pack.

Aaron raised an eyebrow. "Explosives? Seriously?"

"Not explosives," Gil muttered. "Just enough to loosen the seal."

A muffled crack. The ancient stones shifted. A narrow opening appeared.

"One at a time," Gil instructed.

They slipped through the gap, emerging into the shadows behind one of the colonnades near the Dome's western steps.

Ahead of them, the meeting was already beginning.

Midnight – The Society's Gathering

The Dome of the Rock's courtyard was shrouded in moonlight. The air virtually crackled with tension.

Figures stood in a wide circle, tailored suits cloaked in dark robes. Their faces were hidden in shadow, but their presence carried undeniable authority.

Aaron whispered, "That's them."

Gil scanned the group, eyes narrowing. "Get into position. Listen. We need to know who they are."

They moved silently, each taking a different vantage point behind the columns and archways.

Chloe crouched behind a stone ledge, her heartbeat pounding in her ears.

One man—tall, commanding, his voice edged with control—stepped forward.

The Grand Architect.

"The world is no longer ruled by nations," he said, his voice echoing in the sacred silence. "It is ruled by power. And power belongs to those who seize it."

Chloe's breath hitched.

This was bigger than she had imagined.

But then—a sharp noise behind her.

She barely had time to react before a hand clamped over her mouth.

Darkness swallowed her as she was manhandled backwards into inky shadows.

1:00 AM – The Mission Goes Wrong

A commotion erupted.

Gil spun around, catching a glimpse of Chloe being dragged into the shadows by two masked figures.

"Chloe!"

He lunged forward, but suddenly—

The area exploded into movement.

Guards swarmed from every direction.

Aaron, Seraphine, and Luca fought back, but Gil's mind was on one thing only—

Getting Chloe back.

She was gone.

Taken by the very people they were hunting.

The mission had changed.

Now, it was a rescue.

And Gil wasn't leaving without her.

Chapter 11

Grabbed!

The Kidnapping

Chloe had no time to scream before she was yanked backward, a strong arm locking around her waist and a big hand smothering her mouth. She twisted, kicking wildly, her heels slamming into her attacker's shin, but it didn't slow them down.

Panic surged through her veins.

The world exploded into chaos.

Aaron moved first. His military instincts kicked in, his gun already drawn as he fired a shot—controlled, precise. Gil was right behind him, moving like a predator in the dark, landing a brutal elbow into an attacker's face before wrenching a rifle from another.

Seraphine moved with deadly grace. She blocked a strike, drove her knee into a man's stomach, then pivoted, sweeping his legs from under him before twisting his wrist, sending his weapon clattering uselessly to the ground.

Luca—usually the team's joker—was all business now. He grabbed a stun baton from one of the fallen men, cracked it against an attacker's skull, and barely spared him a glance as he collapsed.

Then—Chloe's muffled scream.

They turned, but it was too late.

A hooded figure clamped a cloth over her mouth. She thrashed, clawing at him, but her limbs went weak. The drug worked fast.

"Chloe!" Gil lunged, but a flash grenade detonated, blinding him in an explosion of white-hot light.

By the time their vision cleared, Chloe was gone.

The Escape

More men poured in, their heavy boots pounding against the stone floor. The team had seconds—maybe less—before they were overwhelmed.

Aaron tossed a smoke grenade, filling the room with thick, blinding fog. "MOVE! NOW!"

Luca shoved open a side door, the old wood splintering under the force. Gil stayed behind, his movements lethal, covering their retreat. One last attacker rushed him—he dropped low, sweeping the man's legs, and slammed an elbow into his temple.

Seraphine dragged a wounded Aaron through the door as bullets ricocheted off the walls.

They burst into a narrow alleyway.

A black van screeched to a halt.

"Get in!" Mei shouted from the driver's seat.

No hesitation.

They piled in, and the van roared away, leaving the chaos behind.

But the real fight was just beginning.

Chloe's Interrogation

A splash of ice-cold water jerked Chloe awake.

She gasped, her body shivering violently as she struggled to focus. A dull throb pounded in her skull, the effects of the drug still lingering. The room swam around her—gray walls, dim lighting, the damp scent of concrete and decay.

Her wrists were bound to a chair.

Footsteps.

A man stood before her—tall, sharp-featured, his steel-gray eyes filled with calculated menace.

"Tell me, Chloe," he said smoothly, his voice calm, almost conversational. "Where is the rest of your team?"

She glared at him. "Like I'd tell you."

He smiled, but it didn't reach his eyes. "We have ways of making you talk."

The door creaked open.

Another figure stepped inside.

Chloe's blood turned to ice.

The Society had her now.

Silence in the Safehouse

The moment they returned to the safehouse, the implications of their failure crashed down on them.

Chloe was gone.

Taken right from under their noses.

The room felt emptier without her. The usual banter, sharp wit, and unwavering determination—all of it had been snatched away in an instant.

Gil sat at the table, silent, fists clenched so tightly his knuckles were white.

Aaron paced back and forth, replaying every second leading up to her abduction.

Luca, normally the first to crack a joke, was uncharacteristically quiet, his fingers twitching as he fought the urge to break something.

Seraphine stood near the window, arms crossed tightly. Her expression was unreadable, but her eyes burned with fury.

Lily sat curled in a chair, arms wrapped around herself. She wasn't crying, but her whole body shook with rage and fear. "She always jumps in headfirst," she whispered. "She always thinks she can handle everything on her own."

Dr. Levine placed a firm hand on Lily's shoulder. "Your sister is strong. But she needs us now more than ever. We will find her."

Thalia rubbed at her temples, frustration etched in her furrowed brow. "The Society never takes prisoners without reason. They want something from her."

Aaron spoke first, voice low, controlled. "We should have seen it coming."

"We should have done more," Gil muttered, his voice brittle with anger. "They were right there. Right there."

Seraphine's voice was cold, calculated. "This wasn't random. They planned this. Chloe was the target."

Luca exhaled, running a shaky hand through his hair. "Then we find them. And we take her back."

Aaron grabbed a notepad, scribbling furiously. "The Society is obsessed with secrecy and symbols. They wouldn't just take her anywhere."

Seraphine leaned over the table. "Somewhere hidden. Somewhere ancient. They value places tied to power."

Luca's eyes lit up. "Jerusalem is full of underground tunnels. If they wanted to stay hidden, they could've taken her down there."

Gil stood abruptly, his chair scraping against the floor. "Then we start there."

Aoife, silent until now, spoke with certainty. "I can map the tunnels. If they used them, there will be traces."

Yuki was already working. "And I can track their communications. If they're using encrypted channels, I'll break them."

Dr. Levine adjusted her glasses, thinking fast. "The Society has long believed in sacred geometry and power lines running through ancient sites. If they're using the tunnels, they aren't just hiding—they're positioning themselves."

Lily's fists tightened. "Then what are we waiting for?"

The Search Begins

Hours later, they were moving through the narrow tunnels beneath the city. The air was close and stale, the scent of damp stone pressing in.

Flashlights flickered against the walls, illuminating centuries-old inscriptions in Hebrew and Aramaic.

Seraphine traced a hand over an ancient engraving. "These symbols … they match the ones at the Dome. They must have come this way."

Aaron examined the markings. His stomach twisted. "It's a warning. Something about balance and power. They're following a ritual."

Gil's voice was ice-cold. "Then we don't have much time."

They pressed forward, the tunnels twisting and turning in an unending maze.

Then—a sound.

A low murmur echoed ahead.

Voices. Chanting. The unmistakable cadence of an incantation.

Gil signaled for silence, his hand hovering near his weapon.

They moved in perfect sync, pressing against the cold stone walls, inching forward until the passage opened into a vast underground chamber.

Torches flickered at the center of the room , casting shadows against the rough stone walls.

Hooded figures stood in a circle, their voices rising and falling in creepy unison.

And in the middle of it all—bound and kneeling on the floor—was Chloe.

Her hair was wild, her wrists tied, but her eyes blazed with defiance.

She wasn't broken.

She was waiting. Watching. Ready.

Gil moved first. Aaron and Seraphine followed.

They weren't here for intel anymore.

This was a rescue.

And they weren't leaving without her.

Chapter 12

The Rescue

Chloe's Capture

Chloe's pulse thundered as The Society's hooded figures chanted in unison. Their voices were low and rhythmic, reverberating against the unforgiving walls of the underground chamber. The dim torchlight flickered, sending sinister shadows stretching like skeletal fingers toward her.

The ropes bit into her wrists, but she barely noticed. Her mind was calculating, her heartbeat steadying.

They were performing a ritual—one she suspected was connected to the Seven Seals. If she could just stall them long enough, the team would come.

She had to believe that.

A figure stepped forward, removing his hood. It was the sharp-featured man from before—the one who had interrogated her. His steel-gray eyes bore into hers, amused, patient, deadly. Snake eyes.

"You are not afraid." He tilted his head. "That is either foolishness or arrogance."

Chloe smirked, defiant despite her shackles. "Maybe both."

He chuckled. "You should fear what is to come. The seals were never meant for ordinary hands. Yet here you are, meddling in things beyond your comprehension."

"You're the ones meddling." Her voice was steady. "History doesn't belong to you."

His expression darkened. He reached out, brushing a stray strand of hair from her face.

Chloe jerked back, disgust curling in her stomach.

"You will understand soon enough."

Then—a sound in the tunnels.

A faint echo, barely audible over the chanting.

Chloe's heart leapt.

They were here.

The Team Strikes

Gil signaled silently, his sharp eyes scanning the chamber.

The team had taken out two guards in the tunnels already—quick, efficient work. But this?

This was where things got real.

Aaron gripped his firearm, waiting for the go-ahead.

Seraphine held a blade, poised like a shadow ready to strike.

Luca crouched low, scanning for the best vantage point.

Mei and Thalia flanked the entrance, preparing for the inevitable fight.

Yuki and Aoife stayed at the rear, securing their escape route.

Gil whispered, "On my mark."

The moment stretched, the tension suffocating.

Chloe kept her breathing steady, pretending not to react.

Then—Gil moved.

Everything exploded into pandemonium.

Aaron fired first, the gunshot roaring through the cavern. A Society member dropped before he could react.

Seraphine was a blur, her blade flashing—a slice, a cry of pain, a body hitting the floor.

Luca's stun baton crackled, colliding with an attacker's skull.

Mei, calm and analytical, fought with measured precision. She sidestepped a strike, grabbed an opponent's arm, and flipped him effortlessly onto the ground before driving a knee into his ribs.

Thalia was a storm, weaving between attackers. She caught a punch in mid-air, twisted the attacker's wrist, and sent him crashing face-first into the stone floor.

The Society's ritual shattered.

Gil reached Chloe in seconds, slicing through the ropes with a swift motion.

"Are you hurt?"

Chloe shook her head, breathing heavily. "Let's just get out of here."

Gil hesitated just a second, his hand lingering on her arm longer than necessary. "I wasn't going to leave without you."

Something unspoken passed between them, a connection that didn't need words.

Chloe's pulse skipped, but there was no time to process it.

"Not yet," Seraphine called, dragging a Society member into a chokehold. "We need answers."

The sharp-featured man tried to slip away, but Aaron was faster, tackling him hard.

Aaron pressed a knee to his chest. "Going somewhere?"

The man sneered. "You think you've won?"

"You just lost your leverage." Luca motioned toward Chloe, now on her feet, bruised but unshaken.

The remaining Society members fled, their ritual ruined.

"We don't have time," Gil said. "More could be coming."

Chloe grabbed the nearest abandoned scroll. "Then let's go."

The Escape

They moved fast, navigating the twisting tunnels.

Aoife's voice crackled in their comms. "I see movement above ground. You need to get out now."

"Almost there," Gil responded.

Then—footsteps. Too close.

More Society members, armed and ready.

Aaron turned and fired twice, forcing them to take cover.

"Go! I'll hold them off."

"No." Chloe grabbed his arm, eyes burning. "We all go."

They reached the exit, where Mei was waiting with the van.

The second they broke into the open air, Yuki and Thalia covered their retreat, ensuring no one followed.

Luca slammed the doors shut, and Mei hit the gas.

The van roared forward, the streets of Jerusalem blurring past.

Chloe exhaled, leaning back against the seat.

She was safe.

For now.

The Aftermath

Gil sat across from her, watching her carefully.

"Are you sure you're okay?"

Chloe met his gaze, exhaustion weighing on her, but her determination unwavering.

"I'm fine. But we just cracked open something huge."

She held up the scroll.

"This was worth it."

Gil let out a sharp breath, his shoulders finally relaxing.

"I thought I'd lost you."

Chloe blinked, caught off guard by the raw honesty in his voice.

It wasn't just relief.

It was something more.

Something dangerous.

She swallowed. "You didn't." She held his gaze. "You came for me."

Gil brushed his fingers against her wrist, where the ropes had left angry red marks.

"Of course I did."

Their eyes met, and for a moment, the world outside the van disappeared.

The danger. The mission. The Society.

None of it mattered.

Just them.

Chloe looked away first. "We should … figure out what's on this scroll."

Gil smiled slightly, leaning back, but the warmth in his eyes remained. "Yeah. We should."

The van sped through the dark streets of Jerusalem, carrying them toward the next mystery waiting to be uncovered.

But between them, something had already begun—

Something neither of them could ignore for much longer.

Chapter 13

Deciphering the Scroll

The Safehouse - Unraveling the Mystery

The safehouse hummed with restless energy.

They had scarcely made it back from the rescue, yet no one could rest.

Chloe sat at the center of the table, the ancient scroll unfurled before her, its delicate parchment lined with strange markings that had survived centuries. The edges curled slightly, brittle with age, delicately holding secrets long kept in the shadows.

Across from her, Dr. Levine adjusted her glasses, her sharp eyes scanning the text with focused precision.

Gil stood nearby, arms crossed, his presence steady and reassuring. But every so often, Chloe felt his gaze flicker toward her, checking on her, as if making sure she was really there.

She wasn't sure if it was protective instinct or something more, but she felt it.

That unspoken connection.

That silent promise.

Lily sat beside Chloe, her fingers drumming anxiously against the wood. "I still think we should've brought one of them back."

Chloe turned to her sister. "One of who?"

Lily huffed, exasperated. "That Society member we left behind. He could've given us information."

From where he leaned against the wall, Aaron shook his head. "We didn't have time, Lily. We barely got out of there as it was. Plus, he wouldn't have talked—not willingly."

Luca smirked, arms crossed. "I mean, under the right pressure, maybe. But I agree. He'd have been more trouble than he was worth."

From her spot on the arm of the couch, Thalia nodded, kicking one foot lazily. "The Society members are fanatics. Even if we had dragged one with us, we'd be wasting time trying to break them. Right now, our best bet is the scroll."

Chloe exhaled, running a hand through her hair. "Then let's focus." She pointed at the strange markings running along the edges of the parchment. "These symbols look familiar—similar to what we saw in the tunnels."

Dr. Levine leaned in, adjusting the lamp's angle to cast better light. "They're ancient Aramaic mixed with Phoenician script."

Luca whistled. "Phoenician? That's old-school even for secret societies."

Dr. Levine barely spared him a glance. "The Society believes the seals lead to something powerful. But I don't think they fully understand what they're dealing with."

A Hidden Location?

Aoife traced one of the symbols with a gloved finger, brows furrowing. "This looks like a geographic coordinate."

A ripple of anticipation ran through the group.

Gil straightened immediately. "Where?"

Dr. Levine adjusted her glasses again, her expression becoming thoughtful. "It's not complete, but with the right translations …" she trailed off, then sat back, blinking as if the realization had just hit her.

"We might be looking at coordinates leading to the Negev Desert."

A beat of stunned silence.

Then—

"The Negev?" Yuki echoed, her fingers already flying across her tablet. "Why there?"

Dr. Levine pursed her lips. "That desert holds some of the oldest secrets in this land—hidden cities, lost relics, places that haven't been touched in centuries. If the Society believes something is buried there, we need to get to it first."

Mei, who had been quiet, finally spoke. "What exactly do we think we're looking for?"

Seraphine crossed her arms, her golden eyes glinting in the light. "Something old. Something powerful. And something The Society wants badly."

Chloe studied the scroll again, her mind racing. "We need to move fast. They'll be regrouping after what we did tonight."

Thalia's voice was sharp. "Then we don't waste time. We plan, we go, and this time—we stay ahead of them."

A Shared Resolve

Gil met Chloe's eyes across the table. His voice was quiet but firm.

"We're in this together."

Chloe held his gaze, feeling the weight of the moment.

They weren't just fighting against The Society anymore—they were racing against time, against history itself.

She nodded, her fingers brushing against the parchment.

They were getting close.

Too close.

And the closer they got, the more dangerous this became.

But one thing was clear—they still had a long way to go.

Chapter 14

Journey to the Negev

On the Road - The Desert Beckons

The steady hum of the bus engine droned constantly in the background as the team made their way south, the road stretching endlessly ahead.

Outside the windows, the landscape transformed—rolling hills and rocky plateaus faded into a vast expanse of desert, its golden sands rippling under the relentless sun.

The tension of the past few days lingered, but something had shifted.

Growth. Understanding. A quiet resolve in the face of enormous consequence that hadn't been there when they'd first set out on this mission.

Chloe sat by the window, gazing at the passing landscape. The barren beauty of the desert was calming, yet daunting—an endless sea of secrets, waiting to be uncovered.

She felt the weight of their discoveries pressing on her, but for the first time in days, she didn't feel like she was carrying it alone.

Gil sat beside her, one arm resting along the back of their seat, his presence solid, grounding.

But it was different now—his nearness wasn't just protective, it was something else.

Something unspoken yet undeniable.

"You okay?" he asked, his voice low, meant just for her.

Chloe turned to him, offering a small, tired smile. "Yeah. Just thinking."

Gil tilted his head, studying her. "That's dangerous."

She laughed softly, shaking her head. "You're one to talk."

His usual smirk faded into something softer, something real.

"I meant what I said before." His voice was steady, but there was an edge of raw honesty beneath it. "Back at the tunnels. I wasn't going to leave you."

Chloe met his gaze, her chest tightening.

There was something about the way he looked at her now—like he saw past the armor, past the deflection, past everything she tried to hold back.

"I know," she murmured.

For a moment, neither of them moved.

Then, Gil reached out, his fingers brushing lightly against hers—just for a second.

But it was enough.

A flicker of warmth. A quiet thrill that neither of them acknowledged, yet both felt deep in their bones.

Across from them, Lily saw everything—but, for once, she said nothing.

Instead, she turned to Luca, who was absorbed in the map spread across his lap.

The Plan

Luca tapped his pen against a marked section on the map. "Alright, let's talk logistics. If these coordinates are right, we're heading to Avdat."

Thalia's eyebrows shot up. "Avdat? As in, the ancient Nabataean city?"

From her seat near the front, Dr. Levine nodded. "Yes. It was one of the most important cities on the

Incense Route—an economic and cultural stronghold. And according to the inscriptions on that scroll, it may have been used to safeguard one of the seals."

"Avdat has layers of history," Yuki added, her fingers flying across her tablet. "It was founded in the 3rd century BCE and later flourished under the Nabataeans, Romans, and Byzantines. They built fortresses, bathhouses, even wineries—pretty advanced for a civilization in the desert. But if the seal was hidden there, it has to be in a place that's remained untouched."

Luca leaned back, lacing his fingers behind his head. "So let me get this straight. We're looking for an ancient relic hidden in a city that's been studied by archaeologists for decades?"

He let out a low whistle. "Yeah, sounds easy."

Mei snorted. "Because everything about this mission has been easy."

"Exactly," Yuki agreed, "and if The Society has figured this out too, they could be waiting for us. Again."

Aoife, who had been reviewing topographic maps, frowned slightly. "Avdat has a lot of ruins. If they're searching for something, it won't be in plain sight. We'll need to focus on underground chambers."

Seraphine, leaning against the window with her arms crossed, nodded. "Which means we go in carefully. If The Society is ahead of us, we need to outmaneuver them."

A Team Transformed

Dr. Levine observed them all, something almost proud in her gaze.

When they'd first begun, they'd been a collection of individuals, each with their own skills, strengths, and secrets.

But now?

Now, they moved as one.

They read each other's cues effortlessly.

They trusted each other without hesitation.

"You've all grown," she said, drawing their attention. "When we started this, you were just reacting. Now, you're thinking ahead. This isn't just about solving a mystery anymore, is it?"

Chloe shook her head. "No. This is about making sure The Society doesn't control history. Doesn't rewrite it to fit their agenda."

Gil nodded. "And making sure that whatever these seals really are … they don't fall into the wrong hands."

Aaron sighed, his jaw tightening. "Which means we need to be ready for a fight."

Lily's grip tightened on the notebook in her lap. "Then let's make sure we win."

Dr. Levine gave a small smile, though there was something wistful in her expression.

"Avdat is special," she mused. "The Nabataeans were masters of survival. They turned the desert into a thriving trade hub against all odds. If they saw fit to hide a Seal there, they wouldn't have made it easy to find. We're not just following a clue—we're stepping into a test designed centuries ago."

Quiet contemplation settled over the group at her words.

They weren't just racing against The Society.

They were racing against time. To preserve history itself.

And against the will of those whose predecessors had hidden these artifacts long, long ago.

The Desert Awaits

The bus rumbled forward, carrying them deeper into the vastness of the Negev.

The golden sands stretched endlessly, the horizon wavering under the heat like a mirage.

Somewhere out there, in the ruins of Avdat, lay another piece of the puzzle.

Another mystery was waiting to be uncovered.

Whatever was coming up for them, they would face it together.

Chapter 15

Secrets Beneath Avdat

Arrival at Avdat

The midday sun burned overhead as the team stepped off the bus, boots crunching against the dusty path that led to the ancient ruins of Avdat. The air shimmered with heat, and waves of golden sand stretched far beyond the crumbling stone structures.

Tourists milled about, snapping pictures, their voices a hum of excitement as they marveled at the weathered walls and towering archways—remnants of a civilization that had mastered survival in an unforgiving land.

Dr. Levine adjusted the thin scarf around her neck, taking in the landscape with sharp, knowing eyes.

"I'll stay with the bus." Her tone was firm but not unkind. "Once you retrieve the seal, we'll need to leave fast. If The Society is here, we don't want to waste a second."

Chloe nodded, appreciating the foresight. Dr. Levine was brilliant, but she wasn't a field operative. If something went wrong, they'd need a quick escape.

"We'll be ready." Gil met his aunt's gaze with quiet certainty before turning toward the ruins. "Let's move."

A City of Secrets

The team wove through the ancient stone corridors, the echoes of their footsteps lost in the bustling noise of tourists.

"Alright," Aaron murmured, studying the map on his tablet. "The scroll's coordinates point underground. We're looking for something connected to the Nabataean water systems."

"The Nabataeans weren't just traders," Thalia added, keeping her voice low. "They built advanced irrigation systems to thrive in the desert. If they hid something, it would be near their water supply."

Aoife, analyzing a topographical map, tapped a spot near the acropolis ruins. "There are underground cisterns here. If they were altered in later centuries, archaeologists might have missed something important."

Seraphine crossed her arms. "Then that's our way in."

Finding the Entrance

Beyond the main ruins, the group reached a secluded area where a broken stone archway led downward, partially hidden by collapsed rubble.

Yuki pulled out her scanner, adjusting the settings. "Definitely a hollow space beyond this. We're close."

Luca cracked his knuckles. "Time for some good old-fashioned manual labor."

Gil, Aaron, and Aoife worked together, shifting stones to create an opening large enough to squeeze through.

"I'll go first," Gil said, stepping into the narrow darkness, flashlight slicing through the dusty air.

Chloe followed, heart pounding with a mix of excitement and unease.

The air shifted the moment they entered—cooler, saturated with the scent of earth and time. The walls bore faint carvings, ancient inscriptions half-erased by centuries of neglect.

"This place hasn't been disturbed in a long time," Seraphine whispered, trailing a hand over the stone.

"Then we're on the right track," Aaron said.

Discovery

They stepped into a cavernous chamber with various access points—once a water cistern, now dry and layered with dust.

At its center, half-buried beneath rubble, sat a stone pedestal.

Etched into its surface was a symbol they knew all too well—the same marking was on the scroll.

Chloe's breath caught.

"We found it."

Lily knelt beside the pedestal, knocking away chunks of rubble and brushing away centuries of dust. The carved edges of the stone glowed faintly under their lights, revealing intricate interwoven symbols.

Dr. Levine's earlier words echoed in Chloe's mind.

This isn't just a seal—it's a key.

Gil crouched beside her, his shoulder brushing hers.

"The Society must have known this was here." His voice was quiet but edged with tension. "But they didn't have the full picture."

Chloe swallowed. "Which means we need to figure out how to get it out before they show up."

A sound echoed from somewhere else further down from another of the access points, there had been another entrance perhaps—footsteps. Heavy. Purposeful. Close.

Aaron's jaw tightened. "We're not alone."

Another Confrontation?

Gil instinctively stepped in front of Chloe while Seraphine's dagger glinted as she gripped it tightly.

Yuki's scanner beeped. "Multiple heat signatures. At least five—maybe more."

"They're here." Aoife's voice was calm but resolute.

"We need to move," Thalia said, scanning the chamber. "Now."

Luca bent down, testing the pedestal's weight. "We can carry it together, but we need to go now."

Gil nodded. "Chloe, Lily—you two take the seal itself. Aaron, Seraphine, Luca—help me with the pedestal."

Yuki pressed a small stabilization device against the stone. "I can reinforce it, but it'll be heavy."

The footfalls grew louder.

The Escape

Chloe and Lily carefully lifted the seal, wrapping it in protective cloth.

Gil and the others heaved the pedestal, maneuvering it toward the tunnel entrance. It was heavy, but they pushed forward, step by step, breath by breath.

Seraphine glanced back. "They're coming."

Yuki reached into her bag, tossing a small device into the chamber. "Smoke bomb. Move!"

The room filled with thick gray smoke, masking their retreat.

Footsteps pounded behind them, but the team didn't stop.

They burst into the open, blinking in the harsh sunlight.

Shouts erupted from below.

"Into the crowd," Aaron ordered. "They won't risk exposure."

Blending into the tourists, they made their way back toward the bus, bodies tense, breaths shallow.

Chloe clutched the wrapped seal against her chest, heart hammering.

Gil was beside her, his fingers brushing hers as he whispered, "We did it."

She looked up at him, breathless, adrenaline still buzzing through her veins.

"For now."

As they reached the bus, Dr. Levine was already in the driver's seat, engine running, ready to go.

The doors swung open, and they piled inside, the literal weight of history in their hands.

As the bus roared to life, kicking up a cloud of dust, they knew—

The real battle had only just begun.

Chapter 16

Deciphering the Past

Back at the Safehouse

The safehouse offered welcome respite from the heat and tension from their near escape. Dust from Avdat's ruins still clung to their clothes and skin, and they had returned with more than just ancient dust—it was significant progress.

The ancient pedestal and the newly recovered seal sat on the table in the center of the dimly lit room, bathed in the soft glow of desk lamps.

The team, worn out but resolute, stood around it, their eyes fixed on the intricate carvings on its surface.

Dr. Levine and Thalia were already deep into their analysis, their fingers tracing the symbols etched into the stone with an almost reverent focus. "This is unlike anything we've encountered before," Dr. Levine murmured, brow furrowed in concentration. "The

Nabantaeans were master builders, but this … this predates them."

Thalia flipped through her notes, cross-referencing various symbols. "It's a cipher," she muttered. "A mix of Nabataean script, Aramaic … and something even older. This isn't just a message—it's a puzzle."

Gil leaned against the table, arms crossed, his sharp eyes scanning the markings. "If we can decode this, where do we go next?"

Thalia hesitated, then ran her fingers over a particular marking, her expression shifting from confusion to realization.

Her eyes widened. "Here. This symbol—it corresponds to an ancient reference in the Dead Sea Scrolls."

Aaron leaned forward, gripping the edge of the table. "You're saying the next seal is near the Dead Sea?"

Thalia nodded, excitement flickering in her voice. "And if I'm right, it won't just be hidden—it'll be protected."

Hiding the Seal and Pedestal

Chloe rubbed her temples, her body was exhausted, tugging at her, but her mind refused to slow down.

"If the seal is near the Dead Sea, that means it could be buried in the Qumran Caves." Her voice carried a sense of urgency. "That's where the Dead Sea Scrolls were discovered."

Dr. Levine adjusted her glasses, nodding. "It makes sense. The caves were used to store sacred texts, likely to protect them from Roman forces. If the Nabataeans—or an even older civilization—hid something there, it would've been placed somewhere incredibly secure."

Aaron exhaled, shaking his head. "That also means The Society will be thinking the same thing."

Seraphine's green eyes flickered toward the map. "They might already be there."

Lily and Luca exclaimed in unison, "*Again!*" and burst out laughing.

Gil rolled his eyes, pushed off the table, his stance tense with resolve. "Then we don't waste time. But we must hide what we have before moving forward."

Luca frowned. "You mean stash the one thing they're willing to kill for?"

Aoife nodded. "Exactly. If we're carrying it, we're a target. We need to secure it somewhere they won't think to look. The cave?"

Yuki glanced at her tablet. "No, let's not keep everything together. There's an abandoned crypt beneath an old church nearby. It's locked, but I can get us in."

"That works," Gil said. "We move now."

Securing the Artifact

The team moved under cover of darkness, carefully transporting the seal and pedestal to an ancient crypt hidden beneath a quiet church on the outskirts of town.

The entrance was tucked behind weathered stone walls, untouched by time. Yuki worked fast, disabling the rusted old lock while the rest of the team watched.

The inside was cool and dry, the scent of aged stone and dust surrounding them as they entered.

They placed the pedestal and seal inside a hollow section of the crypt, carefully sealing the opening.

Gil stepped back, surveying their work. "It's secure. No one will find it unless they know exactly where to look."

Chloe let out a slow breath. "Good. Now, let's get some rest before we go after the next one."

A Night at the Guesthouse

By the time they reached the guesthouse, their exhaustion gnawed at every cell in their bodies.

The old stone building stood quietly like an old welcoming friend, its small balconies like smiling eyes, beckoning the weary, the scent of jasmine lingering in the warm air.

Ingrid greeted them at the door, her knowing eyes scanning their tired faces. "You all look like you've been through something."

Lily forced a weak smile. "You have no idea."

"Your rooms are ready," Ingrid said, stepping aside. "I have one ready for your extra guest, as requested. Get some sleep."

The team barely had the energy to respond. They shuffled inside, some collapsing onto couches, others barely making it to their rooms before their weariness pulled them under.

Chloe didn't even remember crawling into bed— just the feeling of sheets against her skin, the distant hum of voices outside, and then …

Darkness.

Morning Departure

The next morning, the team woke early, refreshed but still burdened by the thought of what lay ahead.

The guesthouse kitchen was filled with the usual breakfast aromas of fresh bread and coffee, but no one lingered over the feast this time.

There was too much at stake.

Thalia stood by the window, watching the early morning light stretch over the city.

"We leave now," Gil said, his voice cutting through the quiet.

Aaron had just checked the fuel gauge on the bus. "We're set."

Dr. Levine, who had accompanied them so they could move quickly together as full team, packed up her research notes. "The Qumran Caves won't be easy to navigate, and if The Society is already there, we'll need to be cautious."

Chloe glanced at Gil as they gathered their gear. "You ready?"

His brown eyes met hers, steady and certain. "Yeah. Let's go find the next seal."

The Road to the Dead Sea

As the team piled into the bus, they knew the answers they sought lay ahead—but so did the dangers lurking in the shadows.

And now, The Society was watching. And just as determined as they were.

Chapter 17

Journey to Qumran

The bus rumbled down the dusty road, heading deeper into the Judean Desert. The golden morning sun stretched across the hills, making the sand glow like melted gold. Heat waves rippled in the air, but inside the bus, things were cooler—both in temperature and in the way the group had started to feel more like a team, even a family. They had each other's backs now, no question about it.

Up front, Aaron hummed an old tune as he steered, his hands relaxed on the wheel, while Dr. Levine stood in the aisle, holding onto a seat for balance.

"Qumran is one of the most important archaeological sites in the world," she explained, her voice full of excitement. "Between 1947 and 1956, the Dead Sea Scrolls were discovered in caves there. They were hidden by a Jewish group called the Essenes."

Chloe leaned forward, flipping through her notebook. "The Essenes—weren't they kind of like monks? They lived away from the rest of society, right?"

Dr. Levine nodded. "Exactly. They lived simply, focusing on study and prayer. A lot of scholars think they hid the scrolls on purpose to protect them. Some of the oldest versions of the Hebrew Bible were found there."

She paused, then added, "But before we reach Qumran, I suggest we make a stop at Masada." She glanced around at the group, gauging their reactions. "It's an ancient fortress on a plateau overlooking the Dead Sea, near the town of Arad. Masada is one of the most significant historical and archaeological sites in Israel. It played a major role in the Jewish rebellion against Roman rule in the first century CE. The story of Masada is one of courage and defiance, and when you stand there, looking out over the desert, you can almost feel the history in the air."

Lily's eyes widened. "I've heard about it. Isn't that the place where the Jewish rebels made their last stand against the Romans?"

Dr. Levine nodded. "That's right. When the Romans finally broke through, the rebels chose to die rather than be captured. It's a powerful story, and Masada itself offers breathtaking views and a rare glimpse into ancient history."

Gil crossed his arms, considering. "I agree it's a worthwhile stop."

Aaron chuckled. "It's not a bad detour. And trust me, the view from Masada? Unforgettable."

The group exchanged glances, silently agreeing. They were in. This extra stop would make their journey through history even richer.

Gil, sitting beside Chloe, leaned back, resting an arm over the seat. "And The Society thinks there's still something left to find, right? They wouldn't be interested in this place just for some ancient texts."

Thalia, sitting cross-legged, twirled a loose thread on her sleeve. "Which means the real question is—what exactly are they hoping to find?"

Aaron glanced at them in the mirror, grinning. "You know, you're all missing the *real* important thing about this place."

Lily, who had just taken a sip of water, lowered her bottle and narrowed her eyes. "I already regret asking."

Aaron's grin widened. "I once rode a camel here when I was younger. Amazing experience. Except for one small issue—the camel *hated* me. Kept spitting at me every few minutes."

Seraphine arched an eyebrow. "That sounds personal."

Aaron raised a finger, his expression serious. "The guide told me, 'Camels only spit at people they don't like.'"

For a second, there was silence. Then, the entire bus exploded with laughter. Even Yuki, who was usually quiet, covered her mouth, laughing softly.

Luca, still chewing on a piece of dried fruit, smirked. "So, basically … the camel had excellent judgment."

Aaron clutched his chest dramatically. "Et tu, Luca? I thought we were family."

Chloe shook her head, grinning. "Moral of the story—don't annoy a camel."

The mood on the bus stayed light as Dr. Levine handed out snacks. Aaron had stocked them with everything: cold water, fresh juices, and a spread of Israeli food: soft pita, creamy hummus, crisp cucumbers, dried fruits, and a jar of thick, golden date honey.

Luca ripped open a bag of Bamba and started munching. Mei, always thinking ahead, handed out sunscreen. "Use this," she said firmly. "The desert sun *does not* mess around."

Chloe grabbed a bottle, tossing one to Lily before rubbing some onto her arms. "Last thing I need is to turn into a sunburned tomato."

Without a word, Gil took the sunscreen from her, squeezing some onto his hand before gently rubbing it onto the back of her neck. His fingers were warm, steady, and careful. Chloe froze for a second, feeling a little breathless. She turned slightly, but he wasn't even looking at her, just making sure she didn't burn.

"There," he murmured. "You'll thank me later."

She swallowed, then smiled softly. "I already do."

Outside the window, the scenery was changing. The rolling dunes flattened into a vast, sunbaked expanse, and ahead, Masada's towering cliffs rose like a guardian of the past. The bus pulled into the visitor center, and as they stepped out, the dry desert heat wrapped around them like a thick blanket.

Dr. Levine pointed to the winding path carved into the rock. "That's the Snake Path. It's steep, but it's the way the ancient defenders would have climbed. Or," she added with a small smile, "we can take the cable car."

Chloe wiped the sweat off her forehead. "As much as I love an authentic experience, I'd rather not melt before we reach the top."

Most of the group opted for the cable car, watching in awe as it lifted them over the sprawling desert. The Dead Sea shimmered in the distance, and the higher they rose, the more the fortress revealed itself—massive walls, crumbling storerooms, and a vast plateau that once held desperate warriors making their last stand.

At the summit, silence fell over them. The wind whispered through the ruins, and the weight of history pressed down on them. Lily ran a hand along the ancient stone. "It's … overwhelming," she murmured.

Gil exhaled slowly. "You can feel it. The defiance, the desperation."

Dr. Levine led them to the edge, overlooking the vast desert. "Imagine standing here, watching the

Roman siege engines inch closer every day, knowing your fate was sealed."

Aaron crossed his arms. "And yet, they refused to surrender."

As they wandered through the ruins, the story of Masada came alive around them. They weren't just standing on ancient stones—they were standing in the echoes of history.

The bus hummed steadily along the desert road, carrying them away from Masada, back toward their journey's next destination. Every now and then, they passed groups of Bedouins on camels, the animals covered in beautifully woven blankets, their imperious heads held high like they owned the place.

"Wow," Thalia whispered, watching a group of kids run across the sand, laughing as they played near a colorful tent. "It's easy to forget how much life is in places like this."

Aoife nodded, still staring out the window. "And how much history is waiting to be uncovered."

Dr. Levine adjusted her glasses. "That's why we're here. To find what's hidden—and make sure it doesn't end up in the wrong hands."

The bus fell quiet after that. Everyone understood what she meant. This wasn't just about old scrolls anymore. It was about protecting something important—something that could be dangerous if The Society got to it first.

As the bus neared Qumran, the cliffs ahead grew taller, their shadows stretching over the rocky ground. The sight of them made Chloe's stomach twist—not with fear, but with anticipation.

"Well," she muttered, taking a deep breath. "Here we go."

Gil glanced at her, his voice calm and steady. "Together."

She nodded. "Together."

The bus slowed to a stop, dust swirling around it. One by one, the passengers stepped off, the heat hitting them like a wall. Somewhere beyond those cliffs, something was waiting to be found.

And they weren't about to let The Society get to it first.

Chapter 18

The Hidden Vault

The second they stepped off the bus, the heat hit them like a furnace. The Judean Desert stretched around them in golden waves, the cliffs standing like ancient sentinels, their jagged surfaces whispering secrets buried for thousands of years. The scent of dry earth and salt drifted from the nearby Dead Sea, a sharp reminder that this land was both breathtaking and unforgiving.

Dr. Levine adjusted her hat, already squinting up at the rocky formations ahead. "The Dead Sea Scrolls were found in caves like these, hidden in ceramic jars for nearly two thousand years. If another seal is here, it won't be out in the open. The Essenes were careful and secretive. Whatever they hid, they meant for it to stay hidden."

Chloe wiped the sweat from her forehead and looked

up at the cliffs. "So … where do we even begin?"

Aaron tossed his pack over his shoulder and smiled. "We're climbing."

Lily groaned. "Of course, we are."

Gil, already securing ropes, smirked. "The easiest way to hide something? Put it where most people can't reach."

With that, the team split up. Luca and Yuki stayed on the ground, scanning for underground chambers, while the rest of them tackled the climb. The path was brutal—steep, rocky, and scorching under the midday sun. Loose stones shifted beneath their boots, and every so often, one of them had to grab a hand or steady a slipping foot.

"This is, without a doubt," Seraphine muttered, pulling herself up with a grunt, "the worst idea ever."

"Oh, come on," Aaron called down. "Think of the adventure! The thrill! The—" His foot slipped, and he barely caught himself. "—the mild risk of serious injury!"

"Reassuring," Thalia said dryly.

By the time they reached the cave entrance, they were covered in sweat and dust, but the sight before them made it all worth it. The entrance was narrow, almost hidden in the rock, as if nature itself had conspired to keep it a secret.

Aaron ducked inside first, his voice echoing in the darkness. "Oh, man. You guys are gonna want to see this."

They crawled in one by one, their flashlights cutting through the shadows. Inside, the air was cool, and the walls were smooth as if they had been carved with purpose. At the far end of the chamber, embedded in the rock, was an ancient stone tablet covered in inscriptions.

Thalia stepped forward, brushing dust from the surface with careful fingers. "This isn't just a marker … It's a map."

Chloe exchanged a glance with Lily. "A map to what?"

Before Thalia could respond, Luca's voice crackled over the radio. His usual playfulness was gone, replaced with pure adrenaline.

"You're not going to believe this," he said. "We just found another chamber beneath the ground. And from the scans, there's something inside."

The group felt a jolt of excitement. If two seals were hidden here, this site was much more important than they had imagined.

But the thrill didn't last long.

Aaron's face darkened as he peered back toward the entrance. His body tensed. "We've got company."

Chloe's stomach dropped. Outside, figures moved along the ridge, their silhouettes sharp against the desert sky.

The Society.

Gil's expression was instantly sharp, all business. "We don't have much time. We need to get both seals before they do."

Seraphine was already reaching for her tools. "Then let's move fast."

The team split up again. One group worked to retrieve the seal in the cave, while the other raced toward the underground vault.

This wasn't just a race against time anymore.

The Society wasn't just after history or the seals.

They were after them.

Chapter 19

Race Against Time

As the team moved deeper into the chamber, the cave walls felt like they were closing in. The air was almost suffocating, the visceral scent of time and earth enfolding them like a cloak. Chloe's pulse pounded in her ears as she and Thalia crouched in front of a stone tablet embedded in the wall. Their flashlights flickered, casting shadows that made the ancient carvings look like they were shifting, breathing.

Thalia traced the symbols on the seal with her fingertips, eyes narrowing in concentration. "This isn't just a map …" she murmured. "It's a set of instructions."

Chloe wiped the sweat from her forehead. "Instructions for what?"

"For unlocking the vault below," Thalia said, her voice tight with urgency. "These symbols match the ones

Luca and Yuki found underground. If we don't get the sequence right, we could trigger a collapse."

Chloe's stomach twisted. "No pressure or anything."

Behind them, Gil stood near the entrance, scanning the darkness for movement. Every muscle in his body was tense, coiled like a spring. He turned to them, his voice low. "We don't have much time. The Society is already closing in."

Chloe locked eyes with him and nodded. "Then we work fast."

The Underground Vault

Luca and Yuki had descended into the hidden chamber beneath the caves, their boots crunching against loose rock. The entrance had been buried for centuries beneath layers of sand and stone, but their scanners had picked up something massive.

Aaron, Seraphine, and Mei followed closely, their flashlights sweeping across towering stone pillars. The cavern was enormous, untouched by time—inscriptions covered the floor, and scattered artifacts lay in eerie stillness.

"This is insane," Luca muttered, eyes wide. "It's like stepping into another world."

Yuki's scanner beeped. She turned the screen toward the group. "It's here. The seal."

Aaron stepped forward cautiously, scanning the chamber like a soldier entering a battlefield. "Then let's grab it before The Society does."

Seraphine knelt beside an ancient stone platform, brushing away centuries of dust. As she cleared the layers, golden symbols started to gleam back at them. The same markings Thalia and Chloe were deciphering above.

"We need to wait for the right sequence," Yuki warned. "If we press the wrong symbol, this whole place could turn into our tomb."

Aaron clenched his fists. "Yeah, well, we don't exactly have time to be delicate."

Luca grabbed his radio. "Chloe, Thalia—we need that sequence *now*."

Static crackled, then Chloe's voice came through, breathless. "We've got it. There are three symbols—they need to be pressed in the order of their creation. First is earth—it's a straight line with something that looks like a leaf above it, then water—it's three horizontal wavy lines, then fire—that's two vertical wavy lines with a circle at the top…"

Seraphine inhaled sharply. "Alright. Here goes nothing."

They pressed the symbols one by one in the order Chloe had relayed. The ground rumbled, and a deep, groaning noise echoed through the cavern. Then, there was silence.

Mei exhaled. "Did we just save ourselves or doom ourselves?"

A moment later, the stone shifted. A panel at the center of the chamber slid open, revealing an ancient seal resting on a raised pedestal. Larger than the others they'd found, its surface shimmered with golden etchings. It almost seemed to *pulse* under their lights, like it was alive.

Aaron reached out but hesitated. "Are we sure it's safe?"

Yuki ran a quick scan. "No traps detected."

Aaron exhaled. "Alright then." He lifted the seal from its resting place.

The second he did, the cavern *shook*.

"We need to move," Seraphine warned, gripping Aaron's arm. "Now."

Outnumbered

Above in the cave, Chloe and Gil had just finished deciphering the last markings and dislodging the tablet when the sound of footsteps echoed through the cave behind them.

Gil's eyes sharpened, his hand automatically moving to his side, where he usually kept a weapon. "We've got company."

Chloe's breath caught as she saw figures approaching through the entrance.

It was them. The Society.

The leader—the same tall man with sharp features, dressed in a dark tunic—stepped forward, his piercing eyes locking onto Chloe. "You've found something." His voice was smooth, with a thick European accent. "I suggest you hand it over."

Gil stepped protectively in front of Chloe. "Not happening."

The man sighed like he was dealing with children. "Violence isn't necessary. But if you insist ..."

At his signal, two of his men lunged forward.

Gil reacted first, landing a brutal punch to the closest attacker's ribs. The man crumpled with a wheeze.

Chloe barely dodged another as he swung at her, grabbing a loose rock and hurling it at his face where it hit with a satisfying thunk.

Thalia moved like lightning, twisting out of an attacker's grip and slamming her elbow into his jaw. She grabbed her radio, voice tight. "Aaron, get up here *now*."

Before they knew it, the sound of running footfalls were heard approaching, as Aaron, Seraphine, and Luca had sprinted out of the underground chamber and made their way up to them. Aaron had the seal strapped in his pack.

The Society's men hesitated. They hadn't expected *this* much resistance.

"You're outnumbered," Chloe said, breathless but steady. "Walk away."

The leader studied her for a long moment before he signaled his men to stand down. His expression was unreadable, but his parting words sent a chill down her spine.

"This isn't over."

Then they were gone, disappearing into the desert.

Silence hung in the cave for a long second before Aaron, having arrived, let out a breath. "Well, that was *fun*."

Chloe shot him a glare. "Remind me to *never* go on a treasure hunt with you again."

Gil exhaled, his eyes lingering on Chloe. "You okay?"

She nodded, still catching her breath. "Yeah. Thanks to you."

He held her gaze a beat longer before nodding. "Let's get out of here."

As they trudged back toward the bus, the significance of what they'd found struck them. Two seals in one location. This changed *everything*.

And The Society knew it, too.

Chapter 20

A Moment of Celebration

The bus sped through the quiet roads of the Negev, leaving behind the towering cliffs of Qumran and the lingering effects of the trauma of their latest battle with The Society. The team slumped in their seats, exhaustion a weighted blanket on their spent forms.

No one spoke for a long time.

The two ancient seals were wrapped and secured in protective cases, tucked safely in the compartment beneath their feet. They had won this round, but the war was far from over.

Chloe leaned her forehead against the cool window, watching the desert stretch endlessly into the horizon. Her pulse was finally starting to slow, but a part of her was still humming with adrenaline. They had done it. They had secured history itself.

Gil, sitting beside her, nudged her arm. "We should go straight to the hiding place," he said, his voice low but firm. "The Society won't stop looking."

Aaron, from the seat ahead, nodded. "Agreed. We secure the artifacts first—*then* we rest."

Dr. Levine adjusted her glasses, her expression unreadable. "The cave we've chosen is deep within the Judean Hills. Well-hidden. Untouched by modern hands. This will be the safest place for now."

Aoife unfolded a map, tracing a secluded valley with her finger. "There's an entrance here that leads into an ancient limestone tunnel system. If we store them properly, the seals will be protected from moisture and erosion."

Chloe exhaled, already feeling the anticipation of their next task bearing down on her.

"Let's do it."

The Secret Cave

By the time they arrived, night had settled over the hills, draping the land in silver light. The moon illuminated the narrow path ahead, casting shadows along the rocky cliffs. Armed with flashlights and alert senses, the team moved in silence, carrying their precious cargo through the winding tunnels.

The cave was vast, its walls lined with ancient etchings, whispers from the past carved into the stone. Dr. Levine ran her fingers over one of the markings, her voice barely above a whisper.

"This place has seen history unfold for thousands of years."

They carefully placed the seals into a carved-out alcove, secure in their protective casings. The space felt sacred, untouched by time, as if the cave itself was holding its breath.

Chloe lingered a moment longer, her fingers tracing the rough edges of the alcove. A part of her didn't want to leave.

Gil must have sensed it because he placed a steady hand on her shoulder. "They're safe," he murmured.

She turned to look at him, her blue eyes searching his face. "For now."

He nodded. "For now."

Aaron clapped his hands together, breaking the moment. "Alright, mission complete. Let's get out of here before someone decides to come sniffing around."

A Night in Jerusalem

By the time they reached their guesthouse, the team's energy was sapped completely. The stress of everything they had experienced—and everything still ahead—was engulfing them like a heavy fog.

Gil took one look at their drained faces and grinned. "No way. We're *not* ending the night like this."

Luca groaned into his hands. "Gil, we just *outran a secret society*. Can we *please* just sleep?"

Gil shook his head. "We just pulled off one of the biggest finds in history. We *deserve* a celebration."

Chloe rubbed her temples, amused despite herself. "What exactly are you suggesting?"

"A proper night out. Music. Food. Dancing." His dark eyes gleamed with mischief. "You know, *fun.*"

Dr. Levine, to everyone's shock, chuckled. "There's a place I know. A hidden gem in the heart of Jerusalem, where people from all walks of life come together. Jews, Arabs, Druze, Bedouins—everyone."

Yuki raised an eyebrow. "Is it *safe*?"

Dr. Levine smirked. "Safer than the caves you've been grubbing in."

The Celebration

The restaurant was tucked inside a historic stone building. Its walls were lined with colorful woven tapestries and warm lanterns that cast a golden glow over the space. The scent of sizzling lamb, roasted vegetables, and fresh bread filled the air, mingling with the rhythmic beats of Middle Eastern and Mediterranean music.

A lively band played in the corner, the deep thrum of the drums blending with the hum of conversation and bursts of laughter.

Their table was long, overflowing with steaming plates of food—hummus, baba ghanoush, falafel, roasted meats, fresh laffa bread, and fragrant rice dishes. Sweet mint tea was poured into delicate glasses, and pitchers of locally made wine stood ready for those who wanted a sip.

The tension from the past days began to melt away as they ate.

Luca nudged Lily. "Alright, rookie. Time to dance."

She nearly choked on her drink. "Excuse me?"

He grinned. "Come on. This is *Jerusalem*. You *have* to dance at least once."

Before she could protest, he grabbed her hand and spun her toward the dance floor, twirling her into the growing crowd.

Aaron, meanwhile, had already joined a group of locals in a lively *dabke* dance. He clapped in time with the beat, his enthusiasm making up for his complete lack of rhythm.

Seraphine watched from the table, shaking her head. "He's going to twist an ankle."

Aoife smirked. "Nah. He's got the energy of a golden retriever. He'll be fine."

Chloe sat back, watching it all unfold—the laughter, the music, the way, for the first time in what felt like forever, they weren't running, or fighting, or uncovering ancient secrets.

They were just *living*.

Gil leaned in beside her, his voice low, meant just for her. "See? Told you we deserved this."

She turned to him, a smile tugging at her lips. "Yeah, you were right."

His brown eyes held hers a beat longer than necessary. "I plan on being right about a lot of things."

Chloe felt her breath catch slightly, something shifting between them in that moment. Maybe, just *maybe*, in the middle of all the chaos, something good was beginning.

And for tonight, that was enough.

Chapter 21

A New Mission

Morning sunlight danced through the windows of the safehouse, painting golden lines across the wooden floor. The air was again redolent with the scent of fresh coffee, warm bread, and the fading remnants of last night's celebration.

Despite their fatigue, the team was already gathered around the central table, their focus sharp. There was no time to waste.

Dr. Levine set a thick folder down with a quiet *thud*, her expression grave.

"I received a message early this morning from a trusted colleague—Dr. Elias Ben-Yosef." She exhaled slowly, as if choosing her next words carefully. "He's one of the leading archaeologists specializing in ancient religious relics. And he's issued a warning."

The group stilled.

Aaron, who had been lazily stirring his coffee, stopped mid-stir. "A warning?"

Dr. Levine flipped open the folder, revealing old manuscripts, faded sketches of the seals, and hurriedly scrawled notes in Hebrew. "He believes that uniting all the seals may be … catastrophic."

Silence fell over the room like a weight.

Chloe felt her stomach tighten. "What do you mean *catastrophic*?"

Dr. Levine traced her fingers along the edge of an ancient text. "The seals aren't just historical artifacts. According to Dr. Ben-Yosef, there's an old belief that bringing them together could awaken something. The Society isn't just after power. They're trying to control something far beyond what we understood."

Gil's expression darkened. "So, if we gather them all, we might be handing them exactly what they need?"

Dr. Levine nodded. "That's exactly what we might be doing."

Seraphine crossed her arms. "Then we *don't* let The Society get all of them. Simple."

Aaron leaned forward, his gaze locking onto the map spread across the table. "Where's the next one?"

Dr. Levine tapped a marked location near a shimmering body of water.

"Capernaum," she said. "Near the Sea of Galilee."

Thalia's brow furrowed. "The Society has deep roots there. If there's another seal, it's been *hidden* for a reason."

Yuki studied the map carefully. "How do we find it?"

Dr. Levine flipped another page, revealing an old letter from a historian named Professor Avi Rahman.

"Dr. Ben-Yosef set up a meeting for us with this man. He's been tracking The Society's movements for decades. If anyone knows where the seal is, it's him."

Gil's voice was firm. "Then we don't waste time. Let's move."

Meeting Professor Avi Rahman

The drive north was long but breathtaking. The rugged desert gradually gave way to rolling green hills, the land softening with trees and the distant shimmer of the Sea of Galilee.

When they reached Capernaum, the sight of the water took their breath away. The deep blue stretched out like a mirror, reflecting the afternoon sun. Fishing boats bobbed in the distance, their sails catching the light. Along the shore, remnants of ancient stone ruins stood as silent witnesses to history.

Dr. Levine led the way to a small café near the water's edge. In the shaded outdoor seating area, an older man with deep-set eyes and a face weathered by time waited for them. He wore a linen shirt with the sleeves rolled up, his fingers idly tapping a thick leather notebook.

As they approached, he looked up, his sharp gaze sweeping over them before settling on Dr. Levine.

She stepped forward first, offering a warm but professional smile. "Professor Rahman. It's an honor to finally meet you in person."

Rahman inclined his head, his expression unreadable. "Dr. Levine. I've followed your work for years. I was relieved to hear from Elias. If what he told me is true, you and your team have done what The Society has spent centuries failing to accomplish."

"Not exactly by choice," Aaron muttered under his breath.

Rahman's lips twitched slightly. "Come. Sit."

The team settled at the table as Rahman spread out a collection of old manuscripts, maps, and notes, his movements practiced, deliberate.

"The Society has been searching for these seals for over a thousand years," he began. "But their origins are even older. The seals were never created by a single group. They were gathered over time, passed from one civilization to the next, *scattered* for a reason."

Chloe's fingers skimmed across the pages, her mind racing. "So different people hid them on purpose?"

Rahman nodded. "They were meant to *stay* apart. When brought together, they were believed to unlock something powerful—something that was never meant to be controlled."

Gil's jaw tightened. "Then why has The Society spent centuries trying to unite them?"

Rahman exhaled. "Because they believe that kind of power belongs to them."

Aaron tapped the map. "Where's the seal?"

Rahman hesitated. "There's an ancient structure *beneath* the Sea of Galilee. The Society suspects its location but has never been able to retrieve it without drawing too much attention."

Luca grinned. "Let me guess. We're about to *cause* a lot of attention."

Rahman smiled knowingly. "I arranged a boat for you." He leaned in. "But be warned—if The Society is watching, they won't let you leave *easily*."

Dr. Levine stood. "Then we won't waste time."

But as the others began preparing to leave, she held up a hand.

"I'm staying behind," she said.

Chloe frowned. "What? Why?"

Dr. Levine gave her a reassuring smile. "I'll be waiting near the bus. If something goes wrong, I'll be ready for a *quick escape*." She glanced at Rahman. "Besides, there are things I'd like to discuss with the professor while you're retrieving the seal."

Rahman nodded in approval. "It may be useful. There's much we need to talk about."

Gil didn't look thrilled at the idea of leaving her behind, but he knew there was no point arguing.

"Alright," he said, adjusting his gear. "Let's go get that seal."

The Chase Across the Water

The boat rocked gently as they climbed aboard, the scent of salt and fresh air swirling around them. The sky had begun to darken, a warning that night wasn't far off.

Aaron took the wheel, his grip steady, and guided them toward the coordinates Rahman had given. At first, the rhythmic lap of the water was the only sound, but they were too tense to be lulled by it.

Yuki checked the scanner. "It's here," she confirmed. "Right beneath us."

Just as they prepared to dive, the distant roar of engines cut through the air.

"Company," Seraphine called out, pointing toward the horizon.

Three black speedboats were cutting through the water, heading straight for them.

Aaron cursed. "Well. That didn't take long."

Gil clenched his fists. "We have to get that seal."

Chloe's heart pounded. The enemy was closing in *fast*.

Aaron shoved the throttle forward, the boat lurching as he swerved between waves. Water sprayed into the air as bullets started to hit the sea around them.

Lily grabbed Chloe's arm, her voice tight. "We can't outrun them forever!"

Luca calmly loaded a flare gun. "We don't have to. We just need to make them *regret* their choices."

He fired. The flare streaked through the darkening sky, landing right in front of the lead boat. It swerved sharply, nearly colliding with another. The chaos bought them precious seconds.

Aaron pushed the engine to its limits, speeding toward the submerged ruins.

Yuki's voice rang out. "We need to dive *now*."

Gil turned to Chloe, his gaze intense. "Ready?"

She swallowed hard, adrenaline coursing through her veins. "Let's end this."

With one last glance at the enemy closing in, they grabbed their gear and *jumped*.

The icy water swallowed them whole, muffling the chaos above.

And as they swam downward, toward the ruins lost to time, one thing was clear—
This mission was about to change everything.

Chapter 22

Into the Depths

The moment Chloe, Gil, Yuki, and Luca plunged into the Sea of Galilee, the world above vanished into a haze of rippling light. The water, colder than expected, wrapped around them like an iron grip, sending a shock through Chloe's limbs. She forced herself to focus, regulating her breathing through the mask as bubbles spiraled toward the shimmering surface. Sunlight cut through in golden shafts, flickering against the ancient ruins that sprawled beneath them—remnants of a civilization lost to time.

Gil moved with smooth, practiced ease, scanning their surroundings like a soldier analyzing enemy territory. Yuki checked the readings on her scanner, the soft blue glow casting an eerie shimmer across her diving suit. Luca, naturally, had attached a waterproof flashlight to his wrist, the beam slicing through the murky depths like a sword. His grin was barely visible behind his mask, but Chloe knew him well enough to guess he was loving every second of their deep-sea treasure hunt.

Ahead, the ruins emerged from the sandy depths—massive stone pillars, half-buried in the silt, worn smooth by centuries of relentless water. Moss and coral clung to their surfaces, their edges softened by time but not erased.

Yuki gestured toward a narrow crevice, its entrance nearly lost beneath layers of sediment. With careful hands, they brushed away the murk to reveal markings carved deep into the rock. Chloe's heart hammered in her chest as she traced the symbols—ancient, far older than anything they'd encountered before.

Gil reached out, pressing his fingers against the carvings. The second he made contact, the stone shifted beneath him. A low vibration pulsed through the water, sending a shockwave that stirred the sand into a swirling storm.

Then, the rock split open.

A hidden chamber revealed itself—dark, untouched, and waiting. The seal, resting on a stone pedestal, was there.

Even in the murky water, it gleamed, its golden surface untainted by time. But something about it felt different—more than just another relic. It radiated something ancient, something alive. Chloe and Gil exchanged a glance. Anything hidden this well was never unprotected.

Yuki's scanner beeped.

A trap.

The ground rumbled. Cracks split through the stone. Luca grabbed Chloe's wrist and yanked her back just as a slab of rock came crashing down, sending a cloud of silt into the water, momentarily blinding them.

Gil acted fast, pulling the seal free from its resting place.

Luca's eyes widened behind his mask. He signaled wildly—Time's up. The ruins were collapsing. Gil secured the seal in a waterproof case, strapping it tightly to his back as they kicked hard toward the exit, battling the powerful current now surging through the collapsing chamber.

They burst into clear water just as a dark shape loomed above them.

The Society was waiting.

Back on the Boat

Aaron's voice crackled in their earpieces. "You've got company. Get up here, now!"

Chloe gasped as she broke the surface, yanking off her mask. The boat rocked violently in the waves, its engine roaring as Aaron spun the wheel, dodging an incoming speedboat. The Society's vessels cut through the water like hungry predators, their floodlights sweeping the surface in search of their targets.

Gil hauled himself onto the boat first, then grabbed Chloe's arm, pulling her up. Luca and Yuki followed in quick succession, their movements agile and efficient. The second they were on board, Aaron floored the throttle, sending them surging forward at breakneck speed.

Seraphine braced herself against the railing, her sharp eyes darting from the approaching enemy boats to the soaked team. "Where's the seal?"

Gil unstrapped the case, tossing it onto the deck.

"We don't have time," Aaron growled, swerving hard to the left just as a bullet tore into the water where they had been moments before. "Hold on!"

Chloe grabbed the railing, her knuckles white. "We need to shake them."

Luca was already rummaging through their emergency supplies. He held up a smoke grenade, his grin wicked. "I have an idea."

Before anyone could argue, he yanked the pin and lobbed it overboard. The grenade hit the water with a *plop* before erupting into a thick black cloud that spread fast, swallowing the lake's surface in a choking fog.

"They won't see a thing," Luca smirked. "Genius, I know."

"That won't hold them for long," Yuki warned, eyes sharp as she recalibrated her scanner.

Aaron's jaw clenched. "It doesn't have to. We just need to vanish."

With precision, the team adjusted course, weaving a zigzagging escape route through the smoke. Aaron cut the engine the moment they reached the shelter of thick reeds lining the shore, allowing the boat to drift soundlessly into the shadows.

The Society's boats roared past, lost in the smokescreen.

Silence.

Chloe's breath came in short gasps. The adrenaline was still hammering through her veins, but they'd done it. They'd escaped.

For now.

Chloe nodded, the night air cold against her damp skin, but the fire in her chest burned hotter than ever. Another seal. A mystery that refused to stay buried. A war that had only just begun.

As the boat floated in the darkness, she knew one thing for sure—The Society wasn't going to stop.

And neither were they.

Chapter 23

The Next Clue

The night's still warm air was cut through with the pressure they felt driving them as the team secured the fifth seal. Keeping all the seals together was too dangerous—The Society was relentless. If they found one, the entire mission could be compromised. The team wearily returned to their guesthouse in the German Colony.

Despite their fatigue, sleep refused to come. Adrenaline still coursed through their veins, the intensity of their latest mission playing on repeat behind their eyes. Chloe lay awake, the dim glow of moonlight outside casting shadows on the ceiling as she turned the events over in her mind. Across the room, Lily groaned and flipped onto her side, clearly just as restless.

"This is ridiculous," Lily muttered. "We should be sleeping."

Chloe let out a long breath. "Tell that to my brain."

Lily huffed, throwing a pillow over her face. "Hard to sleep when we're literally holding pieces of history— and The Society is practically breathing down our necks."

Chloe chuckled despite herself. "Yeah, no pressure."

Lily sat up and squinted at her. "We need to knock ourselves out with something."

"Or," Chloe said, shifting onto her side, "we accept that sleep isn't happening and just enjoy a few quiet hours before the next storm."

Lily groaned. "I hate that idea, but you're probably right."

Across the hall, Gil, Luca, and Seraphine were just as awake, reviewing notes and discussing their next move. Mei sat at a desk, sketching out possible routes on a faded map, her pencil tapping in thought. Meanwhile, Aaron and Dr. Levine had gone back to her home, using the time to regroup before meeting them in the morning. Yuki sat by the window, her laptop casting a faint glow as she sifted through encrypted messages from their informants. Aoife leaned against the wall, arms crossed, her mind running a hundred miles an hour.

By dawn, they had long ago given up trying to sleep. The team gathered in the guesthouse's cozy dining area, where Klaus and Ingrid had set out fresh bread, olives, cheese, eggs, and steaming coffee. Despite their sleep deprivation, the meal provided a brief sense of comfort.

Dr. Levine and Aaron arrived shortly after, looking far more rested than the others. Dr. Levine took a seat beside Thalia, sipping her coffee contemplatively, while Aaron wasted no time filling his plate with food.

"Rough night?" Aaron asked, glancing at Chloe and Lily's tired faces.

Lily grunted, dunking a piece of bread into her tea. "You could say that."

As they ate, the Morgenstern's young helper approached their table and, without a word, slid an envelope toward Gil. He then disappeared just as quickly.

Gil held the envelope carefully. The paper felt old, and its edges were slightly worn. The wax seal was unmarked—whoever had sent it wanted to remain anonymous.

Chloe leaned in. "What is it?"

Gil broke the seal and unfolded the letter. The message was scrawled in elegant yet hurried handwriting:

Go to Nazareth. The ancient synagogue. A message will be waiting. It will lead you to Jericho. There, you will find what you seek. But beware—others seek it, too. They are meeting there.

Luca let out a low whistle. "Well, that's not ominous at all."

Dr. Levine's expression darkened. "Nazareth. That synagogue is one of the oldest sites in the region. If someone left us a message there, it means this has been planned for a long time."

Seraphine's gaze sharpened. "And Jericho is one of the oldest cities in the world. If the sixth seal is there, it would also make sense that The Society will be desperate to get there first."

Aoife tapped the table, deep in thought. "Jericho is full of archaeological sites. If The Society is setting up a meeting there, we need to figure out where—and fast."

Mei adjusted her glasses, rereading the note. "They wouldn't risk leaving something like this unless they were certain we'd find it. Which means someone on the inside is helping us."

Yuki, who had been silent until now, frowned. "Or someone is leading us into a trap."

Aaron set his fork down and leaned forward. "Either way, we don't have a choice. We go to Nazareth, find the clue, and follow it straight to Jericho. But we need to be ready. The Society knows we're closing in on the sixth seal."

Chloe met Gil's gaze, her heart pounding. "This is it. We're almost there … only two more to find."

Gil nodded, his expression unreadable. "Then let's finish this."

With that, they rose from the table, leaving behind their unfinished coffee. The chase was on. The sixth seal—and perhaps the answers they had been searching for—were finally within reach.

Chapter 24

Shadows Over Nazareth

The road to Nazareth wound through the rolling hills of Galilee, the golden morning sun casting long shadows across the rocky terrain. The team had left Jerusalem at dawn, packed tightly with their gear into their bus. The air inside was vibrating with expectancy. This wasn't just another stop—it was a message. Someone out there was guiding them, but whether that someone was friend or foe remained unknown.

"Why send us here instead of directly to Jericho?" Chloe asked, her fingers idly tracing the edge of the parchment they had received at breakfast.

"Whoever left this wants us to find something first," Dr. Levine said, adjusting her glasses as she scanned the road ahead. "Nazareth is a place of significance, both historically and symbolically. If The

Society left any traces here in the past, we need to find them before The Society of today does."

Gil, gripping the steering wheel, remained silent, his jaw tight. He was always at his most focused when faced with the unknown, and Chloe knew he was running every possible scenario through his head.

Luca, sprawled in the back seat, smirked. "Well, at least we're keeping things interesting. Straight answers are so overrated."

Aaron chuckled. "Where's the fun in getting where you need to go without a little detour?"

Lily exhaled dramatically from her seat. "You two have a terrible definition of fun."

Seraphine, sitting near the window, was scanning the landscape with sharp, calculating eyes. "Jericho is a war zone in history and mythology. If we're being led there, it means we're about to step into something bigger than just an archaeological dig."

Thalia tapped the map, her voice thoughtful. "And that means we need to be prepared for anything."

Arrival at the Synagogue

Nazareth's ancient district was a maze of stone alleys and bustling market stalls, where the scent of fresh bread and roasting coffee mingled with the aroma of spices. The town was alive with the hum of conversation, merchants calling out, and the rhythmic clang of metalworkers shaping jewelry. It was a place where past and present existed side by side.

The ancient synagogue, a weathered limestone structure that had stood for centuries, was set at the edge of the old city. As they approached, the place's energy shifted—quieter and heavier, as though the walls themselves were whispering of ancient mysteries.

"This place has been here since the first century," Dr. Levine murmured, her fingers brushing over the stone entrance. "Many believe this is where some of the oldest teachings were spoken."

Chloe stepped inside, her boots echoing against the stone floor. Dust swirled in the dim shafts of light filtering through the arched windows, and the air carried the musty scent of old incense, wood polish and time.

"It's empty," Seraphine said, scanning the room with narrowed eyes.

"Not completely," Aoife added, glancing at the walls. "There's something here—we just need to find it."

Yuki, who had been running her fingers over the floor, suddenly stopped at the main altar. "This stone—it's loose."

Everyone gathered around as Yuki carefully pried open a section of the floor. Hidden beneath was a folded parchment, bound with a faded red ribbon.

Gil took it carefully, unwrapping it as the team leaned in. The writing was elegant, yet hurried, as if whoever wrote it had little time:

The sixth seal is near. Hidden beneath the city of palms, where kings once walked and warriors fell. Beware—your enemies are moving faster than you realize. If you seek the truth, you must hurry before it is lost.

"Jericho," Dr. Levine whispered. "The city of palms."

"Someone is guiding us," Chloe said. "But why not just tell us this in the first place? Why send us here first?"

"They wanted us to stop here for a reason," Luca muttered. "Maybe to learn something. Or maybe to be seen."

A sudden noise echoed from the entrance.

Footsteps.

Shadows shifted against the doorway.

"They're here," Gil said quietly, tucking the parchment into his jacket. "Move."

Escape into the Market

The team moved quickly, exiting through a side passage just as voices rose from the synagogue behind them. Chloe's heart pounded as they slipped into the market, where the scent of spiced meats and fresh fruit surrounded them. Merchants shouted over the crowd, unaware of the silent chase unfolding in their midst.

"They were waiting for us," Aaron muttered. "Which means they know exactly where we're headed."

Lily risked a glance behind them. "They're closing in."

Seraphine made a sharp turn. "Then let's make them work for it."

They weaved through the market, moving quickly but trying not to draw attention. Stalls displaying woven fabrics, intricate pottery, and shimmering jewelry blurred past them. Chloe nearly tripped over a basket of dates but kept going, Gil's steady grip on her arm keeping her upright.

A sharp whistle cut through the air—one of the pursuers signaling to the others.

"They're spreading out," Thalia said, her voice tense. "We won't make it back to the bus without being seen."

Yuki's voice was calm and measured. "Then we split up."

Gil's eyes narrowed. "I'll buy us time."

Without waiting for a response, he darted toward a nearby motorbike, hotwired it with practiced ease, and revved the engine. The sudden roar turned heads, including those of The Society's men.

"Go!" he shouted as he sped off, leading their pursuers in the opposite direction.

Chloe and Lily veered left, slipping behind a stall draped in colorful silks. Aaron and Seraphine ducked into a side street. Luca, Yuki, and Mei disappeared down a parallel road, while Thalia and Aoife took a different path, ensuring they weren't followed.

As Gil weaved through the crowded streets, his pursuers close behind, he gritted his teeth and pushed the bike faster. He led them on a winding chase through the alleys, finally losing them near a construction site. Doubling back through a hidden side street, he gunned the motorbike toward the rendezvous point.

The others had already reached the bus, and the moment Gil skidded to a stop, he jumped off, tossing the bike aside before leaping in.

Gil didn't wait. He peeled onto the main road, leaving the city behind, dust swirling in their wake.

Silence filled the bus until Luca let out a slow whistle. "Well, that was fun."

Dr. Levine shook her head. "That was a warning. The Society isn't just looking for the seals. They're watching us."

"They know we're going to Jericho," Aaron said, jaw clenched. "And they'll be ready."

Gil tightened his grip on the wheel. "Then it's time we stopped reacting and started making our own moves."

Chloe looked down at the parchment still clenched in her hand. Jericho awaited them. And whatever was waiting there … was going to spell the end of … whatever this was all about.

The sixth seal was within reach.

Chapter 25

The Lost City of Jericho

The drive to Jericho was tense. The sun hung low in the sky, casting an amber glow over the desert landscape as they sped toward the ancient city. Every member of the team was on high alert, knowing this was it—the sixth seal.

"This city is one of the oldest in the world," Dr. Levine began, breaking the silence. "Jericho's walls have risen and fallen for thousands of years. If the sixth seal is truly here, it's buried deep in its history."

Gil gripped the wheel tightly. "Then we find it before The Society does."

The roads into the city twisted through rugged cliffs and dried riverbeds. The tension in the bus was palpable. They weren't just looking for an artifact—they were racing against—and toward—forces that had been watching them from the very beginning.

Arrival at the Ruins

They parked near the base of Tell es-Sultan, the archaeological site that held the remains of ancient Jericho. Towering mudbrick structures loomed over them, the remnants of civilizations long gone. Tourists wandered the area, snapping pictures, unaware of the true stakes behind this group's visit.

Aaron hopped out first, scanning the landscape. "If I were hiding a relic of power, it wouldn't be in plain sight."

"Agreed," Aoife said, unfurling a map she had been studying. "There are underground chambers here, some undiscovered by modern excavations."

Luca flipped open his laptop, pulling up satellite imaging. "There's a section near the collapsed fortress that doesn't match the rest of the topography. That could be our entrance."

Yuki adjusted her scanner. "I can run a deeper analysis, but we need to get closer."

Seraphine's sharp gaze landed on a series of stone stairways leading down into a trench. "That's where we start."

The Descent into Antiquity

The team moved quickly, weaving through the ruins until they reached the staircase leading underground. It was partially blocked by rubble, but Mei stepped forward, brushing her fingers against the stones.

"These aren't naturally placed," she murmured. "They were set here deliberately—to keep something hidden."

Aaron and Gil worked together to move the heavy slabs, revealing an ancient entryway covered in faded carvings.

Thalia traced the inscriptions with her fingers. "This writing … it's a mix of ancient Hebrew and Aramaic. It speaks of a chamber that must remain sealed, or the past shall rise."

Chloe and Lily exchanged a glance. "That doesn't sound foreboding at all," Lily muttered.

With a final heave, the stone was moved aside, revealing a tunnel leading into the earth. The air inside was laden with dust, the scent of eons of decay filling their lungs as they stepped forward.

The Sixth Seal

The corridor led them into a vast chamber. Its ceiling was lined with intricate symbols that faintly lit up under the flickering beams of their flashlights. In the center of the room stood a pedestal, similar to the ones they had encountered before.

But this time, it was different.

On the pedestal sat not one but two artifacts—the sixth seal, its markings pristine and untouched by time, and a bronze key, its edges shaped like interlocking circles.

"This wasn't just about collecting the seals," Dr. Levine murmured, stepping forward. "The key … it's meant to unlock something."

Before they could examine further, a sharp noise echoed through the tunnels.

Footsteps.

"The Society," Gil hissed, drawing his weapon. "We have to move. Now."

Seraphine grabbed the seal, while Yuki snatched the key. Chloe and Luca worked together to photograph the markings on the walls before Aaron shouted, "They're coming!"

They bolted toward the exit, the sounds of pursuit growing louder behind them.

As they reached the collapsed staircase, The Society's agents emerged, their leader stepping forward—a man draped in black, his face partially hidden.

"You have something that does not belong to you," he said, his voice smooth, dangerous. "Hand it over."

Gil's jaw clenched. "Not a chance."

Without warning, Aaron tossed a smoke grenade, filling the chamber with thick fog. "Go, go, go!"

The team scrambled up the steps, barely clearing the entrance before rocks tumbled down behind them, sealing the passage.

Panting, Chloe turned to Gil. "We did it. We have the sixth seal."

Gil nodded, his gaze locked on the key in Yuki's hands. "Yeah. But now we have to figure out what *that* unlocks."

As they climbed into the bus and sped away from Jericho, they knew this was now deepening the real mystery.

Chapter 26

The Final Seal

The drive away from Jericho was tense, and the nerves of every member of the team were thrumming with the implications of their latest achievement. They had secured the sixth seal and uncovered a mysterious key, but their work was far from over. The Society would not stop hunting them, and now, more than ever, they had to stay ahead.

Dr. Levine's mobile phone rang, shattering the silence. She quickly answered, her voice calm but alert. On the other end was a trusted contact, their voice urgent. "We know where the seventh seal is located. You need to hurry."

She gripped the phone tighter. "Where?"

"It's been hidden at Yad Vashem."

Dr. Levine's sucked her breath in sharply for just a moment before she nodded, composing herself.

"Understood. We're on our way."

She turned to the team, her expression grave. "The seventh seal is at Yad Vashem."

The bus filled with murmurs of confusion. "Where is that?" Chloe asked, frowning.

"It's Israel's Holocaust Memorial and Museum," Dr. Levine explained. "A place dedicated to remembering the millions who perished, to honoring survivors, and to educating the world about the atrocities committed."

Lily's brow furrowed. "Why would The Society hide something there?"

Dr. Levine's expression darkened. "Because The Society has long sought to manipulate history for their own gain. If the last seal is hidden at Yad Vashem, it means they've infiltrated academic institutions, attempting to rewrite truths and control narratives."

Silence settled over the team as the gravity of the situation sank in. They weren't just fighting for the seals anymore—they were fighting for history itself—and the future.

Aaron tightened his grip on the wheel. "Then let's not waste any more time."

With that, the bus roared forward, the road to Yad Vashem stretching out before them, the final confrontation drawing near.

Yad Vashem

The bus pulled into the parking lot of Yad Vashem, the sprawling complex standing solemn and imposing against the Jerusalem skyline. The rest of the team stayed behind as planned while Dr. Levine, Gil, and Aoife prepared to enter. Dr. Levine adjusted her scarf, her face a mask of determination.

"We need to keep a low profile," she reminded them. "No unnecessary attention."

Gil scanned the area, his posture tense but controlled. "Got it. Let's move."

As they approached the entrance, a staff member in a crisp uniform stepped toward them. Dr. Levine stiffened, but the woman merely handed her a folded note, her eyes flicking toward the museum's interior before walking away.

Dr. Levine unfolded the note, reading it quickly. "Hall of Names," she murmured. "That's where we need to go."

Aoife glanced around. "How do we get in without raising suspicion?"

Dr. Levine lifted her museum ID. "I've been here before for research. Follow my lead."

They entered through the main doors, weaving through quiet halls lined with photographs and historical records. The weight of history bore down on them, making every step feel heavier. Rows of haunting black-and-white portraits lined the walls—faces frozen in time, each one a life cut short. Some stared solemnly, others smiling as if unaware of the fate history had in store for them. Documents, letters, and belongings lay encased in glass, fragments of the lives lost.

Dr. Levine slowed her pace, her voice hushed. "Each name, each photograph represents someone who lived, loved, and was taken too soon. This place ensures they are never forgotten."

Gil clenched his jaw, nodding solemnly. "It's humbling. It makes everything we're doing feel even more important."

Aoife exhaled slowly. "It's heartbreaking and powerful at the same time."

They bowed their heads in a moment of silent respect before continuing toward the Hall of Names. As they reached the grand circular chamber, Dr. Levine slowed and scanned the area. A subtle marking on one of the marble panels caught her eye.

"There," she whispered, pointing.

Gil moved quickly, his fingers tracing the edge of the panel. With a slight push, it gave way just enough to reveal a hidden compartment. Inside, nestled among old records, was the final seal.

Aoife exhaled in relief. "Unbelievable. They really hid it here."

Dr. Levine carefully retrieved the seal, slipping it into her bag. "Let's go before anyone notices."

They retraced their steps with practiced calm, exiting the building without incident. As they climbed back onto the bus, Chloe looked up, wide-eyed. "That was fast."

Dr. Levine sat down, her heart still pounding. "We got it."

Aaron didn't waste a second. "Then let's get out of here."

The bus pulled away, the city fading behind them. The final seal was in their hands, but the fight was far from over.

"We need to secure these immediately," Aaron said, gripping the wheel. "We can't keep them all in one place."

Dr. Levine nodded. "Agreed. We'll take the sixth and seventh seal and the key to another safe location. The others remain where they are."

Yuki adjusted her scanner. "I'll run security sweeps once we store them, just in case The Society gets any ideas."

Luca frowned. "Let's make sure we stay at least three steps ahead of them."

They arrived at the next secure location—an abandoned underground bunker deep in the Judean hills. It had once been a military outpost, but now, it would serve a greater purpose. The team worked swiftly, placing the sixth and seventh seal and the mysterious key inside a reinforced vault, locking them away with multiple layers of protection.

Chloe exhaled, staring at the heavy door as it sealed. "For now, they're safe."

Gil met her gaze. "But for how long?"

A Cryptic Warning

Back at the safehouse, the team barely had time to regroup before an urgent knock sounded at the door. Everyone froze. Gil immediately pulled his gun while Aaron positioned himself near the window, peeking outside.

"It's a messenger," Aaron said, relaxing slightly but still wary. "Alone."

Seraphine opened the door cautiously. A young woman, no older than twenty, stood before them, her face partially concealed by a scarf. She handed Chloe a folded note, her fingers trembling slightly before she turned and disappeared into the night without a word.

Chloe unfolded the parchment and read aloud:

They gather in two days at the valley where the river is swallowed by the earth. Time is against you. The Society will soon have all eyes upon them. The last move is yours.

Dr. Levine's expression darkened. "The Society's final meeting."

"That's got to be the Jordan Rift Valley," Aoife said, already pulling up the map. "It's a deep basin which the Jordan River flows through—an area that's been a site for countless historical events."

Aaron leaned forward. "So they really do have a meeting planned. But what do they need all seven seals for?"

Dr. Levine exhaled. "It's not just the seals. It's the key. They must believe it unlocks something of great power."

Mei, who had been reviewing old research notes, added, "If The Society's leaders are gathering, it means they intend to reveal their full plan. They might be looking to use the seals as proof of their control over something much bigger."

A heavy silence filled the room.

"They're going to put on a show," Luca muttered. "A demonstration of power."

Chloe's mind raced. "Then we make sure they never get that chance."

The Final Plan

The entire team huddled, piecing together the details of their strategy. The answer was clear: the seals and the key had to disappear forever.

"We need to take them somewhere no one can access them," Thalia said. "Somewhere beyond even The Society's reach."

Aoife studied the map. "Swiss vaults. Deep in the mountains, highly secure, and nearly impossible to breach."

Dr. Levine nodded. "It's the best option. These vaults hold gold, documents, and priceless artifacts. If we place the seals in different vaults, even if someone finds one, they won't find them all."

Gil leaned back in his chair. "And once they're locked away, The Society's meeting will be pointless."

Luca grinned. "They'll have gathered all their top members just to realize their grand plan is dead in the water."

Aaron cracked his knuckles. "I like it."

Chloe looked around the room, stirred by the moving sense of unity between them all. They had been through so much together—faced death, uncovered history, and fought against a centuries-old force. And now, they had the chance to stop The Society once and for all.

"This is our moment," she said. "We end it here."

Gil's eyes met hers. "Together."

As the team finalized their preparations, the implication of their decision settled over them. The fate of history, knowledge, and power rested on their next move.

The battle wasn't over.

But they were about to make sure The Society lost it for good.

Chapter 27

Dividing the Mission

The morning sun cast soft golden light across the room. Everyone had gathered early, knowing that today was critical.

They had the seven seals and the key, but securing them was only half the battle. Now, they had to ensure The Society could never find them again.

Gil stood at the head of the table, looking at each person in turn. "We can't travel together. It's too risky. The Society is watching airports, borders—maybe even tracking us. We need to split up."

Dr. Levine nodded in agreement. "If you divide into three teams and take separate routes, it will be nearly impossible for The Society to track you all. I'll use my connections to make arrangements with a Swiss bank to store the seals under the highest level of security."

Chloe leaned forward. "How do we make sure no one follows us?"

Aaron, arms crossed, spoke up. "Each team needs a decoy plan—fake destinations, misdirection. You'll take separate airlines, fly to different countries, and only then take your final flights to Switzerland."

The Teams

The room fell silent for a moment before Gil took charge. "This is how we'll split up. Each team will be responsible for transporting some of the seals."

Team One: Gil, Chloe, and Lily. **Team Two:** Luca, Mei, and Aoife. **Team Three:** Thalia, Seraphine, and Yuki.

Dr. Levine and Aaron would remain in Israel, monitoring The Society's movements and keeping communication lines open.

Seraphine raised an eyebrow. "So, each group takes different flights, different connections, and only meets in Switzerland?"

"Exactly," Dr. Levine confirmed. "I've arranged a secure facility in Zurich, deep in the mountains. The vaults are nearly impossible to breach, and only trusted personnel will handle them."

Aoife tapped the map on the table. "We'll each take a different airline, but we need random layovers to throw off any trackers. Once we're in Europe, we'll take a final flight to Switzerland."

Luca grinned. "I like it. A bit of mystery never hurt anyone."

Gil wasn't convinced. "Mystery keeps us alive. The Society isn't going to let this go easily."

Final Preparations

Having successfully retrieved all the seals from their hiding places, over the next few hours, the team packed their supplies, making sure they traveled light but maintained all necessary security measures. Yuki triple-checked their communication devices, ensuring they had encrypted channels to stay in touch.

Lily glanced at Chloe as they fastened their backpacks. "It's crazy, isn't it? A week ago, we were just trying to find clues. Now we're playing a real-life game of espionage."

Chloe smirked. "And we're winning."

Aaron returned with a folder of documents and set it on the table. "Here are your fake passports. I pulled some favors to get these done fast. Your new identities should help keep The Society off your trail."

Dr. Levine picked up one of the passports and nodded approvingly. "This will buy you time. You must stay completely off the grid."

Aaron added, "When you land in Switzerland, a contact will meet you at the airport and take you to the secured location. No one speaks about the seals outside of this group."

Gil slung his bag over his shoulder. "Then let's move. The faster we disappear, the safer this mission becomes."

As they prepared to leave, Chloe caught Gil's eye. There was something about this moment—a sense that, after all the danger and near-misses, they were finally one step ahead. He gave her a small nod, and she knew they were ready.

The mission wasn't over yet.

But they were about to take The Society out of the game—for good.

Chapter 28

The Journey to Zurich

The plan was in motion. The seven seals and the key were divided among the three teams, and soon, they would be out of Israel, leaving The Society chasing shadows. Each group had its travel routes, cover stories, and fake passports. Now, all it had to do was execute the plan flawlessly.

Team One: Gil, Chloe, and Lily – Lufthansa to Munich

As they arrived at Ben Gurion Airport, Gil remained alert, scanning the terminal for any signs of The Society's presence. Chloe clutched her bag tightly, the weight of the three seals and the key resting against her side. Lily, trying to stay calm, kept checking her passport, her nerves barely concealed.

"We'll be fine," Gil said under his breath as they approached security. "Just act normal."

Easier said than done, Chloe thought. As they handed over their documents, she forced herself to breathe. The customs officer barely glanced at them before stamping their passports and waving them through.

Once on the plane, the tension didn't ease. The three sat quietly, watching passengers file in. Chloe could feel Gil's strong and steady presence beside her, while Lily sat by the window, her hands folded tightly in her lap. As the engines roared to life, Chloe turned to Gil.

"Once we land, we move fast," she whispered.

He nodded. "No delays. Straight to our connection."

The flight was smooth, but none of them could sleep. Every glance over their shoulders was loaded with suspicion. When they landed in Munich, they wasted no time navigating the bustling airport. As they boarded their connecting flight to Zurich, relief finally set in. One step closer.

Team Two: Luca, Mei, and Aoife – KLM to Amsterdam

Luca led the way through the terminal with his usual confident swagger, making it look like they were just another trio of travelers. Mei, ever composed, followed closely while Aoife kept an eye on their surroundings.

"You two look way too serious," Luca muttered. "Relax, we're just three friends heading to Europe."

Mei shot him a look. "Two friends and a reckless hacker who likes to talk too much."

Aoife smirked. "Just don't get us arrested before we get on the plane."

Once through security, they settled into their seats. Luca tapped absentmindedly on his armrest, his mind likely running through all the scenarios where this could go wrong. Mei sat motionless, mentally reviewing their plan, while Aoife watched the flight attendants, always observant.

As the plane ascended, Mei whispered, "We should assume The Society knows we're moving. They'll be watching for us in Zurich."

"Then we make sure they never see us coming," Luca said with a grin.

Their stop in Amsterdam was brief, but they navigated it seamlessly. With their second flight secured, they set off for Zurich, knowing that the real challenge awaited them once they landed.

Team Three: Thalia, Seraphine, and Yuki – British Airways to London

Unlike the others, Thalia, Seraphine, and Yuki moved through the airport with a quiet elegance. They exuded an air of confidence that made them nearly invisible— experienced travelers who knew exactly where they were going and why.

Seraphine adjusted her scarf, scanning the terminal. "No tails so far."

Yuki nodded. "Doesn't mean they aren't watching."

Thalia kept her voice low. "Once we reach London, we split for the layover. Different gates, different paths, then meet at the Zurich connection."

Seraphine smiled faintly. "Good plan. Just don't get lost."

The long-haul flight gave them time to rest, but none of them truly relaxed. When they landed at

Heathrow, they moved separately, blending into the crowds. It wasn't until they were safely on their flight to Zurich that Thalia finally exhaled.

"One more leg," she murmured. "Then the real work begins."

Arrival in Zurich

The teams arrived at different times, slipping into the city unnoticed. Dr. Levine had arranged for them to stay at a quiet bed and breakfast tucked away in a small village outside the city.

Gil was the first to arrive with Chloe and Lily, securing their room and making sure everything was in place. The moment Chloe stepped into the cozy interior, the tension in her shoulders eased—if only slightly. When Luca's team arrived next, he walked in with his usual smirk. "Hope you didn't miss us too much."

"Not at all," Chloe replied dryly. "But I was starting to think you got distracted in Amsterdam."

Luca winked. "Only by the scenery."

When Thalia's group arrived last, Seraphine stretched her arms and sighed. "We made it. Now what?"

Dr. Levine's contact was due to arrive in the morning to arrange for the vault deposit. Until then, they had one night to rest, regroup, and prepare for whatever came next.

Gil glanced at the sealed case that held their seals and the key. "We've come this far."

Chloe met his gaze. "Now we make sure they stay hidden. Forever."

Chapter 29

Securing the Seals

The morning arrived, with crisp mountain air drifting through the bed and breakfast's windows. The team gathered in the small dining area, sipping coffee and preparing for the most crucial part of their mission: securing the seals and key in the Swiss vaults.

Dr. Levine's contact arrived promptly at 8:00 AM. He was Franz Heissler, a sharply dressed man in his mid-fifties. He carried an air of authority, his movements precise as he shook hands with each of them.

"I understand you have something valuable that requires absolute discretion," Franz said, his voice low and deliberate.

Gil nodded. "The highest level of security possible."

Franz studied them for a moment before pulling out

a folder. "Everything has been arranged. Your deposits will be split among three of Switzerland's most secure vaults. No names attached, no records beyond what is necessary for retrieval."

Chloe exhaled, relieved. "And the key?"

"The key will be placed in a separate location, far from the seals," Franz assured them. "That way, even if someone gains access to one, they cannot unlock whatever it is meant to open."

Gil nodded approvingly. "That's exactly what we need."

With the arrangements finalized, they set out. The journey into Zurich's financial district was quiet, with everyone deep in thought. Inside the massive halls of the private banking institutions, the air was always cool, and the silence uncompromising. Franz guided them through the process, and one by one, the cases containing the seals disappeared behind layers of reinforced steel.

When it was over, Chloe felt a weight lift from her chest. It was done. The world's most dangerous artifacts were beyond The Society's reach.

A Walk Through Zurich

With their mission complete, the team finally allowed themselves time to breathe. They stopped at a quaint café for a proper continental breakfast—freshly baked croissants, creamy butter, jams, and steaming espressos. For the first time in what felt like forever, there was no immediate danger looming over them.

"This almost feels normal," Lily said, stirring her coffee.

"Almost," Seraphine agreed with a small smile. "Except for the fact that we just locked away ancient artifacts that a secret organization wants to use to control the world."

Luca grinned. "Just another day for us."

After breakfast, they strolled through Zurich's old town, past charming cobbled streets and the shimmering waters of the Limmat River. The city, with its blend of medieval architecture and modern luxury, felt like a world away from the chaos they had left behind.

Thalia took a deep breath, enjoying the crisp air. "It's almost unsettling how peaceful this place is."

Aoife nodded. "Like the calm before a storm."

As they crossed a small bridge, Gil suddenly tensed. Chloe caught the subtle shift in his posture just as a passerby—an unremarkable man in a dark coat—bumped into him. It was quick, barely noticeable, but Chloe saw it.

Gil's hand instinctively reached into his jacket pocket. His fingers closed around a small, folded piece of paper. He pulled it out and read the single sentence scrawled in neat handwriting:

We need your help to stop The Society. Come to Jack and Jo Europaallee tonight at 6:00 p.m.

Chloe's heart pounded. She looked up at Gil, who met her gaze with the same unspoken understanding.

Their mission wasn't over yet.

Chapter 30

The Swiss Enigma Begins

The team gathered in one of the cozy guest rooms at the bed and breakfast, the scent of fresh linen and faint traces of espresso lingering in the air. The note Gil had received sat in the center of the small wooden table, its message clear but mysterious. Outside, the evening air was crisp, the sky darkening as the city of Zurich bustled with life beyond their temporary safe haven.

Gil sat on the bed, his fingers tracing the edge of the note. His expression was unreadable, but Chloe could sense the tension coiled beneath the surface.

"We have no idea who these people are," he finally said, breaking the silence. "For all we know, it's a trap."

Seraphine, leaning against the window, crossed her arms. "But they said they want to stop The Society. If that's true, we might finally have more allies."

Luca, ever the skeptic, ran a hand through his hair. "Or they could be spies, playing both sides."

Chloe exhaled, glancing between them. "Then we go in prepared. We don't reveal anything unless we know we can trust them."

Gil nodded, slipping the note into his jacket. "No weapons, no signs of aggression. But if anything feels off, we leave immediately."

Jack and Jo Europaallee – 6:00 PM

The café was modern yet unpretentious, with large windows looking out onto Zurich's lively streets. The air smelled of freshly brewed coffee and spiced pastries. The four of them entered in pairs, blending seamlessly with the evening crowd.

Two men sat at a quiet corner table. One was older, his silver hair neatly combed, and his sharp blue eyes watched their approach. The other was younger, possibly in his late thirties, with dark hair and a tense posture. Both wore tailored coats, and their presence was controlled but unmistakably alert.

Gil led the way, Chloe beside him, with Luca and Seraphine close behind. As they approached, the older man, Felix, stood and gestured to the seats across from him.

"I'm glad you came," Felix said smoothly, his Swiss accent crisp. "Please, sit."

Hans, the younger man, looked between them warily. "You're being watched," he muttered, barely moving his lips.

Chloe stiffened. "By The Society?"

Felix gave a slight nod. "They know you're here, but they don't know why. Yet."

Gil leaned forward, his voice low but firm. "Then let's not waste time. What do you want?"

Felix exchanged a glance with Hans before replying. "We want to stop them. But we need your help."

Seraphine narrowed her eyes. "Why now? You've been with them for years."

Hans exhaled sharply. "Because we found something. Something even The Society wasn't prepared for."

Chloe's pulse quickened. "And that would be?"

Felix hesitated before speaking. "The Enigma."

A stunned silence fell over the table.

Chloe's mind raced. "What is it?"

Felix leaned in, his voice dropping to a whisper. "It's what they've been after all along. The Seven Seals were only the beginning. The real secret is hidden in the Alps."

Gil's expression darkened. "And you think we can find it before they do?"

Hans nodded. "If you don't, no one will be able to stop them."

The weight of his words settled over the group like a storm rolling in over the mountains.

Their mission wasn't over. It was just beginning.

Thank You, Dear Readers!

Writing this story was pure joy from start to finish. Bringing Israel, the warmth, resilience, and spirit of the people to you was my gift. I truly hope you enjoyed reading it as much as I loved creating it.

Thank you for taking this ride with the amazing Sisterhood Sleuths. Their bravery, wit, and teamwork are the heart of these stories, but your imagination gives them life. It means the world to me that you chose to spend your time with them (and me)!

And the journey isn't over yet! If you're eager for more sleuthing, mystery, and adventure, stay tuned for the Sisterhood Sleuths' upcoming escapades across the globe in 2025. The entire series is as follows:

- *The Obsidian Eye* (Upland, California)
- *The Land of Promise: The Seven Seals* (Israel)
- *The Swiss Enigma: Secrets of the Alps* (Switzerland)
- *Whispers in the Catacombs: Uncovering Naples' Deep Mysteries* (Italy)
- *The Louvre Enigma: Deciphering Codes Among the Masterpieces* (France)

- *The Celtic Mask: Shadows of The Emerald Isle* (Ireland)
- *The Northern Code: Secrets of the Midnight Sun* (Iceland)
- *The Dragon's Awakening: A Tale of Ancient Secrets and Modern Threats* (Japan)

From ancient scrolls to hidden chambers, from icy landscapes to lush forests, Chloe, Lily, and the gang are ready for more mysteries—and I hope you'll join them.

Thank you for believing in this story and its characters. You've made my dream come true, and I'm forever grateful for that.

Until next time, keep your sleuthing skills sharp and your imagination sharper!

With gratitude and a smile,

Cathy Warshaw

Unlock the Secrets!
Become a part of the adventures,
join the Sisterhood Sleuths and receive thrilling
mysteries, exclusive behind-the-scenes content, and a
chance to win incredible prizes!
www.SisterhoodSleuths.net